WHITE MAN WALKING:

*

Selected Stories and Sketches

John Eppel

Mwanaka Media and Publishing Pvt Ltd,
Chitungwiza Zimbabwe
*

Creativity, Wisdom and Beauty

Publisher:

Mmap

Mwanaka Media and Publishing Pvt Ltd

24 Svosve Road, Zengeza 1

Chitungwiza Zimbabwe

mwanaka@yahoo.com

https//mwanakamediaandpublishing.weebly.com

Distributed in and outside N. America by African Books Collective

orders@africanbookscollective.com

www.africanbookscollective.com

ISBN: 978-0-7974-9548-7

EAN: 9780797495487

© John Eppel 2018

DISCLAIMER

All views expressed in this publication are those of the author and do not necessarily reflect the views of *Mmap*.

Acknowledgements

Versions of a number of these stories appeared in the following publications: *Laughing Now* (Weaver Press), *Short Writings from Bulawayo 1, 2, 3* ('amabooks), *The Caruso of Colleen Bawn* and *White Man Crawling* ('amabooks), *Writing Now* (Weaver Press), *Quadrant, Critical Arts, The Warwick Review, BooksLive* (online).

TABLE OF CONTENTS

INTRODUCTION

Many of these stories and sketches are satirical, which means they should not be taken at face value. The author's intention, for the most part, is to attack, via ridicule, those in power, especially political power, who abuse it. Take, 'Who Really Built Great Zimbabwe?', for example: the focus of attack here is not African nationalism, it is the colonial mentality.

Satire doesn't work if it isn't funny, and this, in our politically correct world where telling the truth can be construed as hate speech, is problematic. The traditional role of the clown (or fool) exemplified by characters like Feste in Shakespeare's *Twelfth Night*, was to speak truth to power in a manner which would entertain that power. But, as Feste warns, 'I wear not motley in my brain'. However, this role is being questioned at a time when the class struggle is shifting away from the world's poor to so-called identity politics. Humour has become a trigger warning for those advocates, mainly on university campuses, of inclusivity, diversity, and equity.

The abuse of power in post independent Zimbabwe- as if we didn't have enough of it before that - is not the only theme in this collection. The relocation of power is another, especially how it has played out between the dwindling minority white settlers and the indigenous black majority. Then there is the debatable behaviour of NGOs from the "developed" world, the deeply destructive results of corruption, some shocking outcomes of our *annus horribilis* (2008), *gukurahundi*, and, somewhat bathetically, school teaching.

AN ACT OF TERROR

A baker's dozen of the more committed ZANU PF Women's League were gathered on the stoep of a palatial farmhouse in the Mazoe Valley. The farm, once a highly productive citrus estate, was now used as a weekend retreat by five hundred pounder Amai Pretty Karigamombi-O'Dare. She could shamble, just, but she required the assistance of two powerful bodyguards to lift her into and out of sitting or reclining positions. Her friend, present at this meeting, and wife of the Minister of Spare Parts (Pretty's husband was only a Governor) had ceased walking, but she could still roll and, occasionally, slump. Her name was Lovely Bumbu-McBhambu-Dzvova. The lightest woman there, wife of the Deputy Minister of Workshops, Conferences, and Heroesplushes, weighed in at a pitiful three hundred pounds. To her shame, she could still walk. Her name was Loveliness Vandzihwa

The purpose of the meeting was to help the government sort out its fuel crisis. Food was not a problem. Witness the boxes of Kentucky Fried Chicken and chips that were strewn all over the stoep. Sweetness Chamupupuri had brought out this favourite food of the Women's League in her husband's army helicopter. The pilot had been sent back to Harare with orders to bring out more of the same plus as many crates of coca cola as the helicopter could carry. No, food was not a problem, especially since the government's Operation Murambatsvina had made available to members of the Women's League, Youth Brigade, police, army and other patriotic groups, fruits and vegetables, seized from filthy vendors, at give-away prices. But fuel was a problem,

1

especially now that even members of the Politburo had to leave their Mercedes Benzes at home and seek, shudder, public transport.

The idea came from another half-tonner, Graciouslady Zvambarara-Boomdeeay, wife of a senior CIO operative who may not be named. They had all listened with reverence to the Minister of Fuel Procurement and Vaseline suggesting exciting alternatives like peanut butter, ethanol, and oil from coal. To help them listen with reverence they swathed themselves in metre upon metre of cotton, printed with portraits of our beloved Leader. These bolts of cloth could prove dangerous. Wasn't Pritty O'Tititi expelled from the women's League for not noticing that one of her portraits was upside down? And wasn't Donalbain "pump my tyres" Pombera disappeared for having one of hers in the vicinity of the bums?

Graciouslady got the idea after a drumstick binge, which built up so much gas inside her that she levitated two centimetres above her waterbed. When the gas began to escape, shifting her laterally and then bringing her down to earth, so to speak, she realised its potential as a source of energy for driving tanks, armoured cars, and bulldozers in the government's mission to purge its cities of those ungrateful human maggots, the poor. She it was who designed the plastic gas bags called Vhuvhuta, which the Minister of Fuel Procurement urged the people of Zimbabwe to utilize. At collection points all over the country, modified bowsers were ready to receive gas manufactured in the stomachs of patriotic Zimbabweans. Peasants were encouraged to eat more cabbage, whites to eat more baked beans, and coloureds and Indians to eat more savoury meatballs. And for the nouveau riche, Kentucky fried chicken with chips soaked in tomato sauce, and lashings of coca cola.

The women at the gathering on the stoep of Amai Pretty's farmhouse had volunteered to test a more efficient method of

2

collecting the gas. The experiment was conducted by Joint Operations. The women were attached by means of flexible plastic tubes and rather ticklish grommets to a petrol bowser; and while they chatted away about what geniuses their sons were and what ladies their daughters were; what fun they'd had in Sun City and Dubai; how ungrateful their servants were; which part of the chicken they liked best; how their favourite food of all was chips, the greasier the better... while they chatted and chewed and sucked and shrieked, they manufactured gas and passed it on to the bowser.

That was when the Act of Terror was perpetrated. No one knows for certain who was behind it, except perhaps the only surviving member of those heroic Women's Leaguers gathered, that fateful day, on Amai Pretty's stoep: Percy Ndanga D'ndichiri Fitzkudya-Smith. So huge was she that not even the explosion of the bowser could budge her. The government line was Blair and his gay gangsters. The opposition claimed it was a ZANU-PF set-up. Harare's servile diplomatic community murmured vaguely about Bin Laden and Al Qaeda. But this is what Amai Percy said when I interviewed her at the only section of her Borrowdale mansion that could still accommodate her and her tubs of Kentucky fried chicken and chips with tomato sauce: the helicopter pad. "Ah," said she, "but that day we were having too much farting."

ASHES

They couldn't find a suitable urn so they used a two litre Lyon's Maid "Cornish" ice-cream container. Bukhosi would have appreciated it. That guy had a sense of humour. All his NGO friends and a smattering of locals were there. Icrisati hugged the plastic box to her swagging chest, Mesafi held the poem she had composed for the occasion, Dedi carried the one legged pigeon Bukhosi had accidentally injured on his way down, head first, from the sixth floor balcony of his uncle's apartment in downtown Bulawayo. She was going to release it during the reading of the poem and the scattering of the ashes. "King" George carried the red wine and the crisps, and "Jairos" Jiri carried the meat – don't forget salt and pepper - and the bread rolls. Their plan was that after the farewell ceremony at Efifi they would have a wake, once the Parks Attendants had gone, at World's View. They would build the fire on the mortal remains of Leander Starr Jamieson, store the food and drinks on the mortal remains of Charles Coghlan, and consume them on the mortal remains of Cecil John Rhodes. Bukhosi would have appreciated it. I tell you that guy had a sense of humour second to none.

Early on Sunday morning the chums piled into Dedi's white Toyota 4 x 4, double cab, and Mesafi's electric blue Pajero, and they gunned their engines for the Matopos. What a delightful squash it was: with a frou-frou here, a frou-frou there; here a frou, there a frou, everywhere a frou-frou. Old MacDonald (I wonder if his farm's been designated?) would have been amazed. Past the Churchill Arms Hotel. Past Retreat shopping centre, past the first police road block, and – hooray – we're on the open road. Not being Rhodies, they weren't interested in the greenish hornblende and chlorite schists, which weather into a fairly fertile red clay beloved of the Acacia karroo; nor the yellow-billed kite on the lookout for road carnage; nor that patch of late flowering Rhynchelytrum repens glowing pink in the late autumn light. Honestly, the way these people appropriate the land!

The European girls in the group weren't sure, over which one of them, finally, Bukhosi had killed himself. NGOs, in the spirit of actualizing social democracy, believe that if you've got something good you should share it, and they'd all, at one time or another, taken a bite out of Bukhosi. They found his dreadlocks irresistible. But these sentimental local boys, falling in love at the drop of a G-string; what's with them? That's why Icrisati was going to hang on to the ice-cream carton after Bukhosi's ashes had been scattered. You never know who might be next. Her current lover, Thembani, was starting to look decidedly glum, just because of that fling with Kudakwashe. Christ, it's only a fuck!

Anyway, let's not get morbid now. Bukhosi wouldn't have wanted that. Let's do this thing. And they did it. It was beautiful to behold – except for the blasted pigeon, which refused to metamorphose into any of its symbolic components, whatever they may be. It refused even to spread its wings and soar towards heaven. Not surprising when you consider that it had been smothered in the generalized frou frou (inclining frequently to frottage) of the journey out. The poem, with its refrain of *"super"* (pronounced zoopah), was magnificently declaimed by Mesafi, tears streaming from her eyes, and snot streaming from her nose, and spit streaming from her mouth. Women are such liquid creatures, thought "King" George, as he felt an erection stirring. The

poem went something like this (I can't remember it exactly because...
well... you see... I wasn't actually there), something like:

> Bukhosi, ah, Bukhosi
> For want of a wife
> You taking (sic) your life,
> And we are sad, so sad
> Super Bhukosi.

> Bhukosi, ah, Bhukosi
> We giving (sic) you our "parts"
> But you wanted our hearts,
> And we are sad, so sad
> Super Bhukosi

> Bukhosi, ah, Bhukosi
> Good bye, dear friend
> We missing (sic) you and your "end",
> So sad we are, so sad
> Super, super, super, Bukhosi.

The scattering of the ashes from the summit of Efifi, not far from
the trigonometrical beacon (ugly reminder of Rhodie appropriation)
was positively transcendental. They had miscalculated - O *felix culpa* -
the strength and the direction of the wind up there, and most of
Bhukosi's mortal remains ended up in the hair and on the faces of the
mourners. Icrisati was surprised to find that it tasted slightly salty.

After the ceremony they repaired to the picnic site, waited for the
Parks officials to go home, and then appropriated the "View of the

World", consecrated ground, "and set apart forever to be the resting place of those who have deserved well of their country." *Quatsch!* Dragging dead grass and wood from all over the place, they built a huge fire on the grave of Leander Starr Jamieson who, in death as in life, but no longer sitting, remains at the right hand of Cecil John Rhodes. The fire grew so hot that the brass lid of Jamieson's grave began to blush. NGOs love building fires, the bigger and more destructive the better – perhaps because they are not allowed to build them in their own countries. Once the flames had died down and the red wine was flowing, the chums proceeded to *braai* their steaks and their chops and their boerewors. They hadn't realized how far away from the other grave sites (you've got to keep these Catholics at a distance) Sir Charles Coghlan's had been located, so they decided to use it as their toilet rather than a place to store the food. When the meat was ready they gathered round Rhodes' grave and used it as their dinner table.

What a feast it turned out to be! Zoopah-doopah, they declared. One toast after another was drunk to their late friend, Bukhosi, there in spirit. You could feel his presence in the scent of greasy *braai* smoke, in the texture of gritty bread rolls, in the itch between your legs. And as the night drew on, as the mourners grew a little quieter, nearly time to pack up and return to Bulawayo, to the comfort of their colonial homes, colonial boreholes, colonial swimming pools... above all, to their colonial servants (but don't worry, we're on first-name terms), they made a unanimous decision to repeat the day's events the following weekend, at Victoria Falls. But this time – since the plastic ice-cream carton was empty – it would be a memorial service to Bukhosi, followed by a frolic in the rain forest, a booze cruise, and a gigantic *braai* on the banks of the Zambesi River.

7

AUNTY AUNTY

Doctor Doctor Lisbet Schwartzenshager could not believe her good luck. Just when she thought she'd exhausted everything nasty to write about indigenous white Zimbabweans, she had discovered, in a dusty corner of the Bulawayo archives, in quite the wrong place, tucked away behind a load of Flora *Zambesiaca* junk, the meticulously kept records of one William Package DC Gwanda District. These records covered the years 1950 to 1962, and they contained enough material for yet another PhD. Her Canadian rival and fellow researcher, world famous authority on Southern Africa, co-author of the ground-breaking *ZIPRA: Sex and Death in the Zimbabwean Bush War,* Doctor Bugle Negrapompie, would be jealous. *Ausgezeichnet!* Lisbet would show that Yankee (sic) bitch. They competed for the approval of their mentor, Professor emeritus, Plautus Strange, who, in turn, competed for the approval of none other than that great communist historian, untroubled by Stalin and, in more sentimental moments, happy to quote Brecht:

> We, who wanted to prepare the ground for kindness
> Could not be kind ourselves:

Eric Hobsbawm.

Lisbet's initial PhD thesis: *The Dog Motif in Racist Rhodesia* had been published by Oxford University Press, and had won her many accolades; her second: *White Kaffirs: Investigations into the Racist sub-culture of Pre and Post Independent Zimbabwe* had been published by Cambridge University Press and had placed her among the world's historiographers to be reckoned with. Or, as she preferred to put it, "with whom to be reckoned". This new study would probably push even her gaseous mentor, Plautus Strange, aside.

We are in the year 2005. The last remnants of Zimbabwe's white community (apart from the handful of exceedingly rich businessmen who have sold their souls to ZANU PF) are well and truly down. Lisbet, however, is not prepared to stop kicking. The ones she kicks hardest are the really quite decent - even by German and Canadian standards - teachers, nurses, social workers, receptionists, housewives (and husbands), researchers, journalists, general practitioners, poets, and – the majority – old-age pensioners. It fills Lisbet with disgust and resentment to find that most white citizens of Zimbabwe are not enormously wealthy, enormously cruel, and enormously insensitive; most of them are not tobacco barons, mining magnates, big game hunters; most of them (to misquote the Bard) are, unaccommodated, no more than poor, bare, forked creatures. Of these *Rassistin,* positively the worst are the ones who have been personally kind to Lisbet herself: those who have (r)assisted her with a place to stay, a bite to eat, a story to tell against themselves.

For a shag on a pile of trashy papers written by trashy Rhodesians like D. K. Shone, R. B. Drummond, J. C. Palgrave, E. V. Cook, D. G. Broadley, E. C. G. Pinhey, J. W. Sweeney, Oliver Ransford, Peter Ginn… she got glimpses of their scattered names while being pounded, from above, from below, from the side… thwap thwep thwip thwop thwup… a monologue was beyond her vagina but it could, since the archivist liked it dry, reproduce the five vowels… for a shag and a hundred dollars U.S. in small bills, she was allowed to take the DC's records away with her.

9

"Away" was the home of Kevon and Traycey Kitchen and three children, who insisted on calling Lisbet, much to her private alarm, Aunty Aunty. (Are they mocking me?). Before the local governor and his team of youthful war veterans and middle-aged youths had driven Kevon off his farm, which he had purchased after Independence, he had been Bulawayo's sole supplier of fresh garlic, jalapeno peppers, and globe artichokes. Under the auspices of the governor, the farm became, before dereliction set in – less than a year – a major supplier of firewood and bush meat. Now, since he was capable of doing domestic repairs and minor renovations, Kevon made a living as a handyman. In this he was ably supported by his handywoman wife, Traycey, and his handychildren children, "Chuldrin".

Lisbet first encountered Kevon while she was researching *White Kaffirs*. She wanted to interview him about land ownership and other sensitive Zimbabwean issues. He invited her around for dinner, poured out his heart (and all his booze) to the sympathetic – she called it *Einfühlung* - and very pretty German lady, invited her to stay, and stay she did. She was tired of stale smelling two-star hotels; besides, think of the money she could save! Using the Kitchen's home as a base, Lisbet travelled all over Zimbabwe in her Toyota Land Cruiser, enjoying the hospitality of unsuspecting white families who gave her their side of the story, and used the material, metamorphosed into the jargon of academia, to confirm what the world already knew about so-called Rhodies: that they were lazy, stupid, good-for-nothing, dyed in the wool racists.

To cut a short story shorter, Doctor Doctor Lisbet Schwartzenshager processed the records of DC Package into a dissertation, which earned her a third doctorate. It was entitled: *Scum Rises: White Hegemony in the South-Western District of Matabeleland during the*

Period 1950 to 1962. When the Kitchen family heard of her success, the dissertation was to be published in book form by the University of Chicago Press, they were delighted for her sake, and the children wondered if they should now call her Aunty Aunty Aunty!

BLACK WOMAN BLEEDING

The day I have chosen to tell you about, Ma'gent is the terribilist day of my life. It is the day when they beat me and beat me until they were causing me to menstruate before my time.

Ma'gent, it was the police. They accuse me of MDC. I was asking them for mealie meal. You know they have this new system. They tell you to go buy exercise book – like the school children use. With lines. $70. Hawu! And bring pen. Every day we queue. They stamp our books. No mealie meal today. Come back tomorrow.

But we see the trucks, Ma'gent – full of bags – pum pum. They tell us, no, these mealie meal for Pumula Central or Donnington, or Western Commonage. Then why do they unload these bags? Hawu! We see them. Half the truck they unload and store there by the back

There is a new Officer-in-Charge. She is a terrible lady, Ma'gent Sergeant Jerry. That big one. We see how rich she is, now. How can police send their children to Whitestone and Girls' College? How can police drive Pajero? When we go to house sales to Hillside, she is there, and she buys everything! Curtains, TV, cricket bats, wardrobe, stove, ma'deep freeze, pot plants, carpet… everything! Behind her Pajero you see sometimes five taxis to carry for her. Two boys they hold her money in suitcases. What is happening to our police, Ma'gent? Maye!

That day in the queue I became angry. They said, if you want mealie meal, go and find it in the bush, because you are useless people. Go to England for it. Go to America. I shouted: you have the mealie meal, we know you have it. We know you sell it at Hillside dams, ebusuku, for one thousand dollars a kg. Hawu! This mealie meal was donated by the British and the Americans. It should be for free, Ma'gent. But they make us pay. With what?

Then they arrested me for being MDC. I am not MDC. Me, I am ZAPU. This one called me to come closer to him. He clapped me in front of everyone. Then they dragged me into a room in the charge office. That room, I will never forget it. Sergeant Jerry and three men. They started to strongly assault me with their hands. Then they told me to strip. Everything, even my panties, Ma'gent. I was so ashamed, my God!

They made me to lie down on the cement floor. They fetched sjamboks and wooden logs. They proceeded to beat me all over my body. I was trying to resist so they bound me up hand and foot, and carried on assaulting me for the whole day. They made me roll over and over. Ma'gent, that big lady, she opened my vagina and dropped this hot stuff inside. Then they lit newspapers and burned me all over. Look here, my friend, and here, and here. Look there. These are from newspaper burns. They were pushing sticks up my bums.

When the blood started coming I begged for cotton wool. I was ashamed to menstruate in front of these police. One was calling me a kaffir bitch. They did not give me anything for the bleeding. They just beat me and beat me until I was passing out.

When I woke up I was lying in some bushes by Hornung Park. My clothes were wrapped round my head. Ma'gent I was in such pain! I was just lying there crying for help. That is where you found me. You were looking for a golf ball. Siyabonga. You saved my life. But that was the terribilist day, my God!

BOYS WILL BE BOYS

The scene was set for talks which would redeem hims as weh hhe hartc in hower renamed itself PAPA hPohular Association of Patriotic Ascendantsmwhile the hartc in ohhosition renamed itself uAuuY huemocratic Association of uo or uie YeomenrhA neutral aenue had seen chosen deeh in the South African *platteland*, a holidac resort on a golf course designed sc acolctes of Sol rerzner to cater for the world's wealthiest tourists, who mac se seharated into four categoriesdshorting heroes, film stars, CEOs, and government ministers.

Zimbabwe was on the brink of civil war. The economy had collapsed, and with it the rule of law as well as the once admirable ethical system based on what Kenyans call *harambee*, where the welfare of the community at large takes precedent over solipsists who think that the world exists for their pleasure, a pleasure most frequently located in the belly and the loins.

These talks had to succeed. Both sides had to make compromises in order to establish some kind of power-sharing government that would draft a new constitution, a level playing field, as the politicians like to put it, so that future elections could be free and fair, as the politicians like to put it. A memorandum of understanding had been signed, a mediator from a neutral country had been appointed (an eminent person who dressed and behaved like the stereotype of an English gentleman, paradoxically, because he detested the English). "Shall we begin?" purred the mediator puffing on a Dunhill pipe stuffed with Three Nuns tobacco. His silver grey Saville Row suit exuded a pleasant aroma of English Leather, which blended synaesthetically with the rich caramel of his Chivas Regal whisky, taken not neat, not on the rocks, not with soda, but with an equal measure of tap water. His choice of tipple set the tone, and all the delegates around the table were fondling glasses of the aforementioned scotch: doubles.

14

PAPA: We as the party in power are 'concerned about the recent challenges that we have faced as a country and the multiple threats to the well-being of our people'.

DADDY: We as a two-pronged opposition are in the process of 'dedicating ourselves to putting an end to the polarisation, divisions, conflict and intolerance that have characterised our country's politics'.

PAPA: We are 'determined to build a society free of violence, fear, intimidation, hate...er... patronage, corruption, and founded on justice, fairness, openness, transparency, dignity and equality'.

DADDY: We recognize the 'centrality and importance of African institutions in dealing with African problems, and agreeing to seek solutions to our differences, challenges and problems through dialogue under the auspices of the...er... SADC mediation, supported and endorsed by the African Union....'

PAPA: We are desirous of 'entering into a dialogue with a view to returning Zimbabwe to prosperity'.

DADDY: And we recognize 'that such a dialogue requires agreement on procedures and processes that will guide the dialogue'.

"Good, that's very good," purred the mediator taking a sip of his Chivas Regal and tamping the bowl of his pipe with a horny forefinger. Are you ready to sign?"

PAPA: Not quite. It has come to our notice that our...er...colleagues from DADDY were given the table with the best view in the wine garden.

DADDY: And it has come to *our* notice that our...er...colleagues from PAPA have minibars in their rooms, while we –

PAPA: You have *en suite* bathrooms and-

DADDY: We never get a chance to use the spa because you –

PAPA: Well, what about those girls you were allowed to take into your rooms while we-

DADDY: Shutup!

PAPA: No, you shutup!

15

"Gentlemen, gentlemen," purred the mediator, striking a third match in the serene process of re-lighting his pipe, "let's have another scotch. Waiter! And while we're about it, let's find another venue, a five star resort where you will be guaranteed equal treatment. I know a place outside Jo'burg, which serves the finest champagne in the world. And the waitresses are topless."

DADDY: Bottomless too, I hope. Mine's a double.

There was much mirth at this joke, and as the glasses were re-charged - doubles nudged into trebles - PAPAS and DADDIES shook each others' hands and slapped each others' backs, and playfully punched each others' shoulders. After all, boys will be boys.

BUSINESS IS BUSINESS

They operate at night, like their familiars, the rats and the cockroaches. They come in three colours: brown, black, and white; but there's not it. They are unscrupulous opportunists who care for no one but themselves and, in sentimental moments, their children – possessions, after all. They take comfort in Jesus' words out of context: "The poor always ye have with you": as only those without the compassion of Jesus can.

In the still hours, after the dogs have stopped yapping, but before the first cocks begin to crow, listen. You'll hear a sound of grumbling, a suburban belly-ache of a sound. It's the thirty ton trucks laden with the scarcest of commodities: cement, sugar, maize meal, cooking oil, petrol... It's not easy for these monsters to negotiate driveways that were designed for motor cars, bicycles and pedestrians; but they manage. They knock down road signs, maim trees, mangle street lights, collapse culverts... but they manage. Let a poverty stricken street vendor dare to be caught with an unopened packet of sugar and she will face the full wrath of the law. The sugar will be confiscated and the woman, probably a grandmother, will be beaten senseless.

But these ruthless exploiters of the suffering poor are safe; safe behind their concrete walls and sheet iron gates, dotted all over suburbia, as far away as possible from the Central Business District and the Industrial Sites. Each one enjoys the patronage of a cabinet minister or a governor or a high ranking officer in the army. Ask the local police to investigate these nocturnal goings on and they will decline. These are, after all, political matters.

And if you ever manage to get in touch with one of these wheeler-dealers – you'll find him at church, at the club, on the golf course, on

17

the Board of some NGO, at so and so's wedding anniversary, at such and such a fund-raising event... but not in queues, never in queues – if you ever manage to get in touch with one, and ask him why, he'll give you a boyish smile and say, "Business is business."

Not for Satisfaction Gomarara your bulky commodities like cement and mealie meal. He needs no thirty ton truck to transport the product that is rapidly making him one of the richest men in Zimbabwe. His BMW is quite adequate, thank you very much. Don't tell anyone, but Satis, as his clients like to call him, has a Swedish girl friend – well, not really a girl friend, they screw occasionally but they don't go out on dates – who works for the United Nations World Health Organization. Her job is to distribute ARVs to the many thousands of impoverished AIDS victims in Zimbabwe. And guess who (WHO) helps her distribute the drugs? Yes. And the Swedish lady, Valhalla Spunkstrom, trusts him, trusts him implicitly. Why shouldn't she? It would be downright racialistic for a white woman to mistrust a black man, especially when he's been intimate with her. Valhallah still blushes with pride when she remembers the hundreds of kronor their sponsored fuck raised for the Entumbane Old Peoples' Home that rainy day in Stockholm, only minutes after she and Satis had met for the first time.

He lives down the road from me. I sometimes see him emerging from his sheet iron gate pushing a pram imported from Spain, which can be adjusted into a push-chair or a feeding chair or a cot. Satisfaction is clearly devoted to the contents of this protean wonder, as, item, four lips indifferent brown; item, four brown eyes, with lids to them; item, two necks, two chins, and so forth. Yes: twins. At other times he emerges with a pair of the largest, most vicious-looking dogs I have ever seen: Great Dane cross boerbull, with a hint of Irish wolf hound. More frequently I have seen him behind the wheel of a custom-

18

made, roofless land rover accompanied by two very beautiful girls, one white, one brown. His, it seems, is a binary world. And you'd be surprised how young he is.

Among Satisfaction's clients, no fewer than thirty have names, which are proceeded by the title: "honourable". Many more are preceded by honorifics, which denote rank in either the civil or the armed forces. At least one is a "His" something or other. Most of the others may be classified by the euphemism "Company Director". When Valhallah Spunkstrom had entrusted her fun-loving friend with the distribution of ARVs throughout Zimbabwe she briefed him on the particular need of impoverished women who now make up two thirds of the Zimbabweans infected with HIV. They have no power to stop their husbands (who frequently have multiple partners) from forcing sex on them without using condoms; no power to prevent transmission of the virus to their babies since they cannot afford breast milk substitutes; no power to help avert the shocking prediction that by 2010 there will be, worldwide, 25 million children orphaned by AIDS. Satisfaction produced the correct facial expressions during the briefing to reassure the warm-hearted Swede, and she sent him off with a genital squeeze and the first of many boxes full of Anti-Retro-Viral pills.

The first box earned him enough money to move into the house down the road from me. The second box earned him enough to surround it with concrete walls and electrified wire, and God knows what other security features. Then came the vehicles, the dogs, and many other accessories like pretty ladies, a lawned verge, and children. One Sunday morning I passed him on the road outside his gate. He was dressed in a powder blue safari suit, which did not conceal an incipient paunch. The chubby twins, one in either arm, were gurgling with contentment. We greeted each other, then I made a gesture towards his property and said, disingenuously, "How do you do it?"

He gave me a boyish smile and replied, "Business is business."

DISCARDED

The s niaersitc of f uhane is a stretch of ohen fieldhlt was here in the Month of Mac, 200i that hANs PF officials held a *pl nt we* hresided oaer s c Senior Assistant hommissioner Hahhcs oc z aaah He told the eHhausted aillagers that, according to the constitution, onlc a war aeteran could s e made president of "our sovereign nation." Whenever he used the word "sovereign" he dabbed his plump cheeks - all that pork roast - with a white hanky, in the style of Kenneth Kaunda.

Attending the meeting was ardent ZANU PF supporter, Willibald Nyoni. At 30 years old he was the proud possessor of 20 hectares of land, part of a white "owned" farm, which the *Third Chimurenga* had restored to the indigenous peoples of Zimbabwe. For three months Willibald had lived like a king: meat, beer and girls; day after day, night after night. Then the firewood ran out; suddenly Willibald was destitute: no meat, no beer, no girls. For the second time in his life, Willibald was rescued by the government. They offered to feed him and perhaps even pay him for services rendered, in short, to help the war vets and the militias terrorize opposition supporters.

"Never again will we be a colony!" shouted the Senior Assistant Commissioner. (It seemed that the higher echelons of government shared the same speech writer.) "We are a sovereign entity." Dab of hanky. "Let Brown and Bush beware! Let that homosexual across the border beware! Let puppet sanctions-mongers beware! We are of the fist!" At this point he incongruously waved his hanky. "If His Excellency, R. G. Mugabe, does not win the run-off, there will be conflict in our sovereign land [dab, dab]: black against black. You must defend the revolution; otherwise we will go back to the bush and fight." He was sweating profusely even though there was a chill southeaster blowing from Johannesburg. His belly was so huge - he found pork crackling irresistible - that he had to wear his belt around his bum.

"Democracy is only for the educated. There is no day on which this sovereign [dab, dab] country will be handed over on a silver platter. How can we give power to those who have no knowledge of governance and no support from you, the local voters, but has (sic) support from puppets and homosexuals?" He went on in this manner for hours.

The next speaker was a war veteran (much too young to have fought in the *Second Chimurenga*) called Comrade Hotstuff. He was armed with an AK 47, which became an improvised guitar in a dance routine that combined *toyi-toyi* and *kwasa-kwasa*. When he began to speak, the rifle was restored to its original purpose, and he discharged a few rounds into the air - to revive audience attention. "Be warned: the soldiers are watching to see the polling station returns. *Pasi na* Tsvangirai!"

"*Pasi.*"

"For every MDC vote in this constituency one of you will be shot dead. *Pasi na* Brown!"

"*Pasi.*"

"Remember *Gukurahundi!* We have lists of MDC supporters. We know who you are! *Pasi na* Bush!"

"*Pasi.*"

If you want to die, if you want to have your homesteads burnt down, go ahead and vote for that puppet of the west, Tsvangirai! *Pamberi na* Mugabe!"

"*Pamberi.*"

"*Pamberi ne* sovereignty!"

"*Pamberi.*"

"*Pamberi ne* Operation Vote Wisely!"

"*Pamberi.*"

Comrade Hotstuff then called upon voters to surrender their MDC cards and T-shirts, and gradually a small pile of these items grew at the size thirteen boots of the war vet. A youth wearing a ZANU PF T-shirt arrived with a tin of paraffin and a box of matches - and the pile was soon blazing merrily.

Willibald Nyoni was assigned to a group of militias from Mashonaland who had recently been deployed to the region. Their brief was to intimidate the rural folk into voting "wisely"! Since he was native to that area, Willibald was given the task of providing the militia with meat, beer, and girls. This he did with commitment and enthusiasm. His greatest achievement, which earned him high praise, not only from the militias but from none other than Comrade Hotstuff, who partook of the subsequent spoils, was to commandeer an ox from the kraal of a successful re-settled farmer, indeed a neighbour and distant relative, Ndabazinhle Nyoni. Single-handedly Willibald drove the ox to the abandoned primary school where the militias had set up a torture centre, slaughtered it, gutted it, and skinned it. Then he chopped it into workable pieces and shared it out. Single-handedly he rounded up willing (i.e. hungry) girls, and a forty gallon drum full of opaque beer. What a feasting was there that night, what hanky-panky, well into the next day! Willibald Nyoni became a hero of the Struggle. *Aluto continuo.*

The strategy set up by Joint Operations Command worked: His Excellency R. G. Mugabe was voted, unopposed, back into the driving seat, so to speak. Now loyalists like Willibald who had done the dirty work for the Party, were no longer required; indeed they had become an embarrassment. What was Willibald's surprise when, a few days after the presidential run-off, three policemen armed with batons arrived at his plot and arrested him for stock theft? In court he admitted he had taken the ox as part of the continuing struggle. He was providing for patriots who were defending his beloved country from the evil machinations of the west. The magistrate, without once looking up, sentenced Willibald, without right of appeal, to nine years in jail, a veritable death sentence.

EMPTIES

Vusi sold grass brooms at the Hillside shopping centre. He was twelve years old and he should have been at school. He was employed by Mrs Ruchiva who bought the brooms and other grass products from peasants in the communal lands beyond the Matobo hills. These she sold in Urban Bulawayo at a hundred thousand percent profit. She had to contend with inflation. To keep overheads down, Mrs Ruchiva employed so-called street kids. They were paid on commission: one percent of all the money they deposited into the crocodile skin hand bag that emerged, open-jawed, from the tinted, electronically lowered window of Mrs Ruchiva's prowling Mitsubishi Pajero.

One evening, while Mrs Ruchiva's hand bag was receiving Vusi's takings for the day, she spoke: "Vusi, you are my best seller. I need someone to deliver meat all over town. This job carries a regular wage, and I would like to offer it to you; but first, you must get a bicycle.

"I will try to get a bicycle, Madam."

"You have until the beginning of next month."

Vusi went back to his spot outside the Hillside KWIKSPAR dreaming about owning a bicycle.

He was about to "close shop" for the night when a sleek black Mercedes Benz with government number plates turned into the shopping centre. It stopped right next to Vusi. Down slid the driver's window revealing a most distinguished looking gentleman with a shaven head and gold rimmed dark glasses. "Do you want a job, kid?" said the gentleman.

"Yes please, Sir."

"Are you a hard worker?

"I am, Sir."

"Right. I've just purchased a property nearby, Lysander Avenue, and I have already found tenants who want to move in on Monday. My problem is that the garage is packed to the roof with rubbish. Can you get rid of it all over this weekend?"

"Yes, Sir." Vusi's heart was thumping. Perhaps he would earn enough to put down a deposit on a bicycle.

"Very well." He handed the boy two keys. "The large one is for the main gate, and the little one is for the garage. Can you find 43 Lysander Avenue?"

"Yes Sir."

"Good. I don't care what you do with the rubbish. Just get rid of it by Monday. I'll pay you in pula or rands once you've given me back the keys."

"Thank you, Sir."

The property was a block from Vusi's *kia*. He decided to start working immediately.

The previous occupier had been an elderly white man who had died of unrequited righteousness. He might have decided to live longer if he'd been aware of the value of the inflation-defying empties that had accumulated in his garage. All street kids knew the value of empties. They spent much of their waking lives searching for discarded beer or coke bottles.

Vusi couldn't believe his luck. Not only were there hundreds of empties in the garage but they were in crates, which made them a lot more valuable. All night long he carried crates to his *kia,* and all weekend he dug, with a borrowed shovel, a pit in a corner of the property where he buried the contents of the garage, mainly cardboard boxes full of Rhodesian memorabilia.

By Monday the garage was spotless and the gentleman swopped his keys for 10 rand in small change. Over the next week, Vusi claimed the deposits on his empties at various outlets in town, and he made enough money to buy a Raleigh Bomber with two inch rims and a large metal carrier attached to his front handlebars. It would be perfect for meat deliveries.

FIVE WITH ONE BLOW

It wasn't the fact that Ravine Boyo-Davis was a downtrodden African American, or a woman, a lesbian at that, or a left-hander, which prompted her to kill, in historical order, an Italian, an Englishman, a Dane, and a Frenchman. It was her Welsh name, which connected her to the original inhabitants of the island now known as Great Britain. She was a true Briton; the rest (and deep down she included Jamaicans and Pakistanis) were colonials.

Ravine bridled at the thought that the word "Welsh" actually meant "foreigner" in the language of the Anglo-Saxons. They made me a foreigner in my own land, she bitterly mused, (this notwithstanding the fact that she had been born in Memphis, Tennessee). My African brothers and sisters complain about being colonised... *hullo*... what about me? Not once, like the Africans, but four times!

First those bastards the Romans; forced us to speak Latin; polluted our dear land with towns, villas, theatres, public baths, central heating - roads, for pity's sake! Then, one morning, they pull out, leave us high and dry, easy pickings for those damned Anglo-Saxons who force us to use disgusting words like "tit" and "bum"! My ancestor, King Arthur, and his merry men, fought so bravely against those barbarians, but to no avail. Next thing there are smelly farms all over the place, and ships choking up the sea, and monasteries making booze out of honey, and literature. That *Beowulf* is un-bloody-readable. Next come the Danes, raid after raid - raping, rioting and looting - and that idiot, Canute, who thought he could make the sea obey him. But worst of all for Ravine Boyo-Davis were the Normans. That William the Conqueror regarded her motherland as his own personal property. How dare he, with his Doomsday Book and all! Bloody frog! Forcing us to speak French. All those stupid castles. And war! war! war!

She spent fruitless weeks searching downtown Memphis for an Italian, an Englishman, a Dane, and a Frenchman so that she could settle her score with the colonial oppressors. Then she heard that Africa was teeming with NGOs from all over Europe. She had once spent a year on Rotary Exchange in a dump of a place called Bulawayo in Zim-something-or-other. She would re-connect with some of her Rotary "parents", find a place to stay, and then settle some scores.

She was so obsessed with her mission that she failed to notice how the once gracious Bulawayo Airport had dwindled to a corrugated iron hangar. She did notice, however, that Mr Wallop (call me Wally), her erstwhile "dad", had, in twenty years, undergone a remarkable transformation: his bum had disappeared into his tummy, and his tummy made normal hugging impossible; so they simply shook hands.

"How are you otherwise...er... Ravine?" Were his first words to her.

She was fine and looking forward to her research. She had explained to "mom" and "dad" Wallop, by email that she was working on her PhD thesis, the working title of which, "Race, Gender, and Left-Handedness in Homophobic Postcolonial Societies", impressed them very much.

By the time they had passed through the third police road block, both feeling thoroughly grubby after being repeatedly body-searched for diamonds, emeralds, and gold nuggets, Ravine Boyo-Davis was in possession of information, which was likely to make her mission a ridiculously easy one, and all thanks to Wally, who was in one of his more confessional moods.

She'd asked him if he knew any NGOs (which he didn't) but that got him talking about his own pedigree. "You know, Ravine, I'm a third generation Rho...er... Zimbo, but I can trace my line back to four different countries."

"Really...er... Dad?"

"Call me Wally."

"Really, Wally?"

28

"Yes. Let's see, now... my maternal grandfather was Italian, a Paraffini... he married a Danish girl, name of Kierkegaard... my paternal grandfather was English... John Wallop, and he married into a French family, the La Normandies... very posh, they were...."

It was like winning the lottery, hearing each number coming out slowly, each one correct. Ravine's heart began to pound. And there was a bonus. Her Rotary "dad" was a coloniser in his own right, a coloniser of her African brothers and sisters. Five with one blow. And she wouldn't have to cut his throat. In his condition she could simply pop him.

She asked him to stop the car so that she could take a photograph of Bulawayo's cooling towers. Instead of a camera, she removed from her back-pack a switch blade cunningly fashioned to look like a harmless vibrator. Then she leaned over to the unsuspecting coloniser and released the blade into his tummy. Hot air smelling of stale Castle lager escaped in a series of sighs, which forced the avenger to look quizzically at the seeming vibrator in her hand. Wally Wallop said nothing but his face took on a confused look as it proceeded to crumple. She opened the driver's door and pushed the withering balloon on to the road. Then she drove back to Joshua Mbaqanga Nkomo Airport, just in time to use her return ticket to North America via Johannesburg. Luckily for her there was one spare seat - in Business Class.

GOAT SONG

I was chatting with my friend, Clair, who is a Researcher for an NGO based in Bulawayo. She is working on a project to improve goat production for subsistence farmers in the more arid regions of Matabeleland. Her research takes her to some very remote areas where hunger and disease have become endemic.

Clair is also interested in literature and, on that particular evening in early September, the air rich with the scent of grass fires and syringa blossom, a bottle of local red wine and a plate of raw carrots (Clair's favourite snack) on the table before us, we discussed Ireland's contribution to English literature. I pointed out jokingly that without the Irish and the gays (occasionally combined) there wouldn't be much English literature to speak of. Even the Bronte sisters were half Irish. The conversation somehow got on to the playwright J. M. Synge, and his one-act tragedy, *Riders to the Sea,* which I had studied at university. I remembered our lecturer telling us that the life expectancy of fishermen on the Arran Islands was so brief that their coffins were built prior to their drowning. In the play, Maurya loses her husband and all six of her sons to the sea. I can still quote her haunting words: "holding a thing in the half of a red sail, and water dripping out of it". The story prompted Clair to tell me of an incident, which she had encountered on a recent trip to the Nkayi area of Matabeleland. I banished the twilight from our glasses and she began.

"We came across this old woman, thin as a stick with bright, almost demented eyes, and a body permanently stooped in the posture of hoeing. Her compound was near Dakamela, on the Shangani River, and she was the sole remaining inhabitant. She told us that both her daughters had died-"

"Of AIDS?" I interrupted.

"Of AIDS and hunger. Her daughters and all her grandchildren. And her six sons had crossed the Limpopo to South Africa. This old woman was barely surviving on green pawpaw fruit and a pod, which she called ihabahaba-"

"That's monkey bread. Piliostigma thonningii. She must have been desperate."

"Yes, but the surprising thing was that she owned twelve healthy billy goats: six black and six white. We asked her why she didn't sell a couple of them in order to buy food, and she said they were not for sale; they were for her son's funerals. She was convinced that all their deaths would precede hers.

"I assumed that the goats would be used for ritual purposes. You know, there is an inkubalo rite, which is performed a day after the burial. They kill a goat, mix it with herbs, and say a protective spell over it. Then they roast the meat and one by one the mourners take a bite of it, while the inyanga knocks their joints. This helps strengthen the family by driving away the fear of death, and bad luck in general."

"I thought they used an ox," I said, munching on a sweet, juicy carrot.

"They do, the ingovu, but how many people own oxen these days? Then there is another ceremony called umbuyiso, which takes place before the rains start a year after death – stop crunching that carrot in my ear!"

"Sorry."

"At sunset a goat is slaughtered, roasted, and eaten, just by the family; but before that it is taken to the grave and offered to the dead person-"

"To appease him?"

"Yes; and to persuade him to come home. It is driven back from the grave and killed. What the family don't eat is left in a hut along with a calabash of beer and some snuff so that the spirits can feast and drink."

"So that was two goats for each son?"

"Yes. I don't know how she kept them so healthy. There was not a blade of grass for miles around, and very little foliage on the trees and shrubs. I've never seen such devastated land."

"Isn't that what goats do?"

Clair bridled at my suggestion. She is an agronomist who knows her livestock, goats in particular. "It's simply a matter of husbandry," she sniffed. "In any case, what ruined the land were generations of forced overcrowding because of the Land Apportionment Act and other draconian Settler policies."

"You're right, there, Clair," I replied; "put it this way: you aren't wrong."

She told me to grow up, playfully stuffed a piece of carrot in my ear, took a sip of wine, and proceeded with her story. "Anyway, we commended the old woman for sticking to tradition in these terrible times, and you know what she said?"

"What?"

"She said it had little to do with tradition. The goats would be bartered to pay for her sons' coffins. She had already ordered them from an Undertaker in Bulawayo, who had promised to deliver them to her door, so to speak, in return for the twelve goats. She showed us an elevated position where she would store the coffins, safe from termites.

"One of our translators who'd stayed on to do follow-up work got back yesterday, and I asked him about the old woman. He said the coffins had arrived and the goats had gone. He'd helped her secure the coffins from termites, but what they hadn't taken into consideration were the ZANU-PF militia, the so-called green bombers. These teenagers had secured a cow from a peasant farmer who had failed to deliver his meagre crop of mealies to the Grain Marketing Board, and were now looking for firewood to roast the beast. They accosted the old woman and demanded to see her ZANU-PF membership card. When she couldn't produce one they beat her senseless and then ransacked her compound.

"That night all six coffins went up in smoke."

Have you ever choked on a piece of carrot? Thank God Clair knew how to execute the Heimlich Manoeuvre. In her arms at last!

HOME SWEET HOME

When Grant Terrier heard that his father, Foxie, and last remaining relative in Zimbabwe, had died at the Edith Duly Home for the elderly, he decided to revisit his past, and attend the funeral for which, since his grandfather had become destitute, he had to pay. All Zimbabweans who relied on pensions to support them had become destitute, and those who weren't kept going by the Western Union simply turned their faces to the wall and died. Very few actually drank insecticide or packed their grizzled heads in SPAR plastic bags and left them there. Most simply stopped living.

When James "Foxie" Terrier retired in 1995 his monthly pension amounted to the princely sum of $10 000. He was rich. He was a paid up member of the Bulawayo Golf Club. He had accounts at Haddon and Sly and Highfield Pharmacy. Once a week he dined out at Maxies or New Orleans. What more could an old man want? Ten years later that same monthly pension bought him one third of an English cucumber.

Grant was A Kitchener High old boy, so his first trip down memory lane, after the funeral, was to that august institution, in a Bulawayo suburb called Lobengula. Grant had played first team cricket and hockey, but the sport at which he had excelled was squash (he still proudly wore his Colours blazer on special occasions), and Kitchener High was the only school in Bulawayo, which, in those days, boasted a squash court built to international standards. The funding had been provided by a deeply committed Parent-Teachers' Association.

Grant decided to walk from the suburban Guest House where he was staying, and this partly prepared him for the shock to come. He made his way along cycle tracks, which had become obstacle courses, and diagonal dirt paths strewn with litter by the bin full. There were as many crows in the sky than there had been storks in his school days; as many rats in the grass than there had been hares. A smell of damp ash lingered in his nostrils.

School was in session when he got to the main gate. The same sign, barely legible on a surface of rust and dents and peeling paint. Hundreds of children were milling about, unsupervised but well behaved on what, in Grant's time, had been called the Top Field. It was now a dust bowl. So was the Oval, the erstwhile First Team cricket ground. Except for a few curious looks from idle pupils, Grant was able to wander about the grounds uninterrupted. Memories flooded his consciousness, the unpleasant ones taking him somewhat by surprise. Top Field was where fights took place, and where new boys had to run a gauntlet of leather cadet boot laces, wet towels, and stockings filled with sand. Top Field was where, Saturday after Saturday in the miserable winter term, the pupils, dressed in their Number Ones, were obliged to watch rugby and scream war cries until their throats ached and their straw-bashered heads pounded.

Only one of the eight tennis courts was still operational, and that, barely. The all-weather surface was cracked and potholed, and the white markings had virtually disappeared. (He remembered the hours he had spent over weekends playing ball-boy for the terrifying prefects). On either side of a pitiful rag of a net six boys, three to a side, were having great fun with a single smooth – cracked, if the low bounce and hollow sound was anything to go by – tennis ball. The Olympic size swimming pool looked as if it had been empty for many years. There were certainly many generations of frogs, rats, chameleons, lizards and beetles, decayed, dead, and alive, on its cracked and peeling floor. Grant quickly pushed aside a memory of being almost drowned there by a serial bully from Shabani whose name he did not care to remember.

While Grant was shaking his head at the once magnificent school hall, now in a sad state of disrepair, a gentleman dressed in a tailored three-piece suit approached him and asked if he could help him in any way. While Grant explained his business, the gentleman withdrew a white handkerchief of a silken texture from his trousers pocket and proceeded to dust his Italian-style leather shoes. His hair, Grant noticed, was sleek with Vaseline, and on the second finger of his left hand was an onyx inlaid gold ring. Dapper was the word that occurred to Grant Terrier.

The gentleman returned the handkerchief to his pocket and then held out his hand for Grant to shake – the African way – which always caught Grant unawares, resulting in a bungle, and that made him feel vaguely guilty. "You see," said the gentleman, "things are far much better now."

"But-"

"Our schools are open to everyone; not the privileged few. We are now having democracy. All are equal."

"But why is everything so run down, Mr O'Magate? I mean, check this hall. When was it last painted? And what's happened to the swimming pool, the tennis courts, the playing fields…?

The Headmaster smiled patiently before replying. "Money, you know, is in short supply. There have been successive droughts. Your people – Blair… Bush – have imposed sanctions on Zimbabwe. They are punishing us for giving the land back to its rightful people. We are struggling against an imperialist conspiracy to keep us subjugated."

"The farm invasions took place only a few years ago. Kitchener High school looks as if it hasn't had any maintenance since Independence."

"That is an incorrect statement, but however, this is not the time for quarreling, Mr Grant. Perhaps you, as an old boy, will find a way of acquiring paint for our buildings."

"Some years ago I sent a thousand Australian dollars to the school for the express purpose of maintaining your squash court. I'd heard that it was being used as a lavatory. You spent the money on a workshop!"

"By the way! Ah, but it was before my time. That must be Mr D'Mpofu, who is now late. But you are wrong about the squash court, Mr Grant. It has been converted into a cottage for our Maintenance Engineer, Com... er... Mr FitzNcube."

Grant asked the headmaster if he could look around his old hostel, Arsenal House. Mr O'Magate, distracted by the arrival of a beautiful young woman (teacher? parent? secretary?) with an exposed navel and a Cleopatra style hair piece, gave his permission, and Grant wandered over to the place that had been his home for six years.

Only the first three letters of the proud old name could be made out; and the word "house" had lost its "s" and part of its "u", so now it read "hole". Grant had been Head of House in his final year. He wondered through what had been the junior prep room. A few photographs of boys and staff still clung dustily to the walls, including one of his first year at Kitchener High. There he was, twelve years old, looking like a frightened rabbit. He recalled most of the seventy odd faces including the serial bully from Shabani. What was his name? Some of the old tables were there still, around which the boys had not studied for many a test, not completed their homework assignments,

37

not written letters home; but had carved their names, splashed ink, and fiddled with sharp instruments.

After some searching he found his grandfather's name, "Yorkie", dated 1914. Then he found his father's name, "Foxie", also dated: 1939. At last he found his own name, so deeply carved that the "S" in "Staffie" had gone right through the table top. It was undated. His surname was incomplete: "Terr". The hostel master had caught him in the act, and beaten the living daylights out of him. "I hope this will teach you a lesson, young Terrier," he had said before commencing the onslaught.

"That I must not vandalise government property, Sir?"

"No. That you must not get caught!"

When Grant "Staffie" Terrier walked pensively away from his alma mater, he was accompanied by the words of a song, not from his own lips, though he had sung it often as a child, but from the school choir, which had assembled in the quad outside the dilapidated hall, and which was being conducted by no less a personage than the headmaster, Comrade "Mister" O'Magate:

Mid pleasures and palaces though we may roam,
Be it ever so humble, there's no place like home;
A charm from the sky seems to hallow us there,
Which, seek through the world, is ne'er met with elsewhere.
Home, home, sweet, sweet home!
There's no place like home…

Not very tunefully, Grant picked up the refrain… "no place like home…there's no place like home…."

INSERTIONS ON ASSEMBLY DAY

T he Headmaster was pushing a cube of ice up his bum to soothe his piles. He was lying over his desk, on the reception side, with his pants down (no underwear, mind you), and his legs splayed, when in walked his secretary calling, "Knock, knock!"

Doris 'Busybody' Jinks had once been obliged to attend a "show" at one of Bulawayo's more sleazy nightclubs, and the part she had found most disgusting of all was a dance routine where an ...er... oriental-looking lady shot ping pong balls out of her fanny. Now this! The Headmaster had already lost three cubes of ice to the regions of his enlarged prostate gland; here was a fourth. The surprise entrance, office left, of Mrs Jinks, and her subsequent shriek, caused him to lose concentration, and out shot two unmelted suppositories, one connecting with the ornate plastic frame of his secretary's spectacles (Mr Vesuvius F. Crakc would not tolerate an Americanism like "glasses" in his office), the other bouncing harmlessly off one of the many sporting trophies that adorned his sanctuary. Both cubes ended up on the highly polished parquet floor where they gradually melted into tiny puddles.

"Now look what you've done!" shouted the headmaster whose face glowed with three intensities of redness: embarrassment, anger, and natural. "You've gone (he pronounced it 'gorn') and stained my floor!"

"Well, what about my glasses?"

"Your what?"

"My... er... specktickles."

"Spect-UH-kills!"

"Sorry, spict-AY-culls."

These damn Rhodesians, thought Vesuvius, who considered himself British (certainly not Zimbabwean) through and through. Hadn't he fought for King and Country against the blasted Hun? And

39

didn't he have a shrapnel wound in his neck to prove it? Nobody had to know that it had been an accidental discharge. He had been on guard duty, somewhere in the Western Desert, those bitterly cold, star-infested nights, with a full magazine and one in the spout. Then he had to masturbate, didn't he - those long-lashed camels, refractory, lying down in the melted... er... melting.... Moral of the story: don't pull your wire with the safety catch off!

"They cracked!"

"What?"

"My gl... specs... they cracked. Look."

"Quite frankly, Mrs Jinks, I don't give a damn. Why don't you ever knock?"

"I did. I said, 'knock, knock'. There's news, Mr Crakc, news!"

"What news? Don't get cryptic on me, Mrs Jinks. I know you spend valuable office time poring over the Chronicle crossword."

"If it's so valuable, why do you pay me so little, hey? Why?"

"I have no control over your stipendium, Mrs-"

"Well then, the Bawd."

"Why don't you ask the Board? You seem to be banging half of them!"

"Ah big yours!"

"You heard what I said. Now, what news?"

"You not goween [She dropped her Gs as sheep drop droppings] to get away with this, Mr Crack! Jis' becawse you so old, hey!"

"It's 'Crakc', not 'Crack'!"

The headmaster was well past retirement age. One of the few advantages left of having a white (for Mr Crakc, read "brindle") skin was that white-owned or white-administered institutions like Private schools, Sports clubs, and Safari camps employed you, hospitalisation and/or senility notwithstanding, till death you them part. "What news, Mrs Jinks?" He knew that his secretary's urge to gossip, to spread rumours, to nudge, nudge... wink, wink, was more powerful than any other urge, even hanky-panky with random board members, random sports masters, and random ground staff.

"There's been a murder on the premises."

"I beg your pardon?"

"A murder, Mr Crakc, on the premises."

Adverbs and pronouns beginning with the twenty-third letter of the alphabet shot out of the headmaster's mouth like ping pong balls. He suddenly remembered that his trousers were still down - Mrs Jinks was staring at his mangled willy. Hastily he pulled them up and then went through the fumbling process of buttoning. He refused to countenance zips, not only because they were new-fangled but because they had been invented in Sweden, a country he abhorred. He regarded them as Nazi collaborators. He tucked in his shirt, cursing under his breath the shortness of its tails, buckled his belt to the last notch, he was losing weight, and gave his full attention to his secretary.

"The new art teacher, you know, the one who wears flour bags to school."

"Miss Reedbuck?"

"Mizz. She's a feminist."

"Even in death?"

"Ah big yours?"

"Go on."

"On the rugby field - sometime last night-"

"How?"

"Pencil."

"Pencil?"

"HB. The red and black kind."

"Staedtler."

"Ah big yours?"

"The pencil, you idiot. It's a German make. Blasted Hun. Clearly we didn't give him a sound enough drubbing in the Last Effort."

"'Last effort'?"

"The War, damn you!"

41

"Don't you talk to me like that, you old goat. Wait till my husband-"

"Your husband would congratulate me. Now, tell me more about this murder? How do you kill someone with a pencil, unless you ram it up the bum, Tshaka Zulu style."

"That's what they did. Rammed it up her... er... bottom."

"But a pencil is too flimsy. It would snap. Discomfort yes, even pain... but death?"

"Maybe the tip was poisoned."

"That would do it. Curare, perhaps."

"How can she be cured when she's dead?"

"Not 'cure', you blithering idiot, 'curare'."

"Don't shout at me, Mr Crakc!" She turned to go. When she walked, her stockings rubbed against each other and made a sound like Christmas beetles. "You better get to assembly; the bell went ages ago."

"Do you think I should announce this news to the school?"

Mrs Jinks stopped at the door and turned again, patting her over-lacquered hairdo: "How should I know?" she pouted, "after all, I'm only a secretary, aren't I?" She stalked over to her desk in the adjoining room, which she shared with the bursar, an Afrikaans lady with a gammy leg whose favourite expression was "I nearly frekked, jong!" (loosely translated as "I nearly died, hey!"), and who wrote short stories in her spare time, meaning office time.

"Yissus, Doris, I nearly frekked when It came to me." She was rummaging in her left ear with a cotton bud.

"What, Vergina?" (for that was the name of the Treasurer of the Budding Writers Association: Vergina Sidestitch.) "Do you mean the murder?"

"Ja. I mean, why her?"

"Because you don't like her. You jealous of her. She sells her paintings. You haven't sold one of your stories."

42

"It's true, I don't like that show-off bitch, and I resent the fact that she's so often absent, like today, but I'm not jealous of her, Doris. She makes pictures for chocolate boxes; I write about real issues."

Doris Jinks returned to her Chronicle, neatly folded at the crossword puzzle. The matrix was almost completely filled in. "Here's one for you, Vergina: 12 across, 14 letters: blank, blank, blank, blank, S,I,M,I,L, blank, blank, blank, blank, E."

"What's the tlue?"

"'You need four eyes to see that the drivel of this muse only appears to be real.'"

"Well you've got four eyes, Doris. By the way, what happened to your dlasses?

"Cracked. You won't believe what I caught the headmaster doween! And the old goat really swallowed it."

"You naughty, Doris, you know that?"

"Ag it's jist a bit of fun, man. Have you worked it out?"

"Those stupid tlues are always anagrams."

"'Appears to be real' must be the definition, so the anagram words are 'drivel' and 'muse'."

"And the letter 'i' occurs four times. This is a tough one."

* * *

Six hundred girls and boys, ranging from the ages of five to twelve, were crowded into the school hall waiting for assembly to begin. Their teachers sat, facing them, on the stage. At the approach of the headmaster, the crowd parted like the Red Sea for him to pass through its midst. In his wake, with straight backs, flaring nostrils, and neatly brushed hair, came the head girl and the head boy. In his attempts to stride to the stage, Vesuvius careened dangerously, first to the right, then to the left, and this caused much flinching and cowering among the pupils on the edge of the divide.

One of the teachers, Mrs FitzTitz, Grade 5 F, offered the headmaster a hand up the three steps that led to the stage. He dismissed her with a shrug and a, "Go off, I discard you!". He caused some confusion when he got to the podium, flanked by the head girl and the head boy, and called out "Please stand!" The pupils were already standing. To cover up for the gaffe, he decided, as if it had been part of his plans, to make a game of it. "O'Grady says, please sit?" He waited until every single child had managed to sit in that cramped space. Then he called, "O'Grady says, please stand?" Once every pupil had resumed the standing position he leered (he had never learned to smile) and said, "There, that was not too difficult, was it?" There came a muted, slightly staggered "No, Sir" in reply.

"Bow your heads to pray," said - no, not the headmaster, but the head girl. "Lighten our darkness, O Lord, and by thy great mercy, defend us from all the perils and dangers of this night... er... day... amen."

"Amen." Muted and slightly staggered.

Then it was the head boy's turn. He opened the Bible he had been carrying and read: "The reading is taken from Deuteronomy, Chapter 25, verses 9 and 10. 'Then shall his brother's wife come unto him in the presence of the elders, and loose his shoe from off his foot, and spit in his face, and shall answer and say, so shall it be done unto that man that will not build up his brother's house.

'And his name shall be called in Israel, the house of him that hath his shoe loosed.' Here ends the reading." The head boy closed his Bible and looked expectantly at Mr Crakc.

The latter thought for a while, cleared his throat, and addressed the assembly in stentorian tones. "Now, what lesson do we learn from the reading?" A few hands went up but they were ignored. "We learn, boys and girls, that you should make sure your shoelaces are properly tied, in order to prevent accidents. Now I want you to look down, and if you see any shoes that are loose or untied, spit in that child's face. Do it!"

They did it, and the spitting commenced. The headmaster allowed it to go on for a few seconds and then called out, "That will do!" The spitting stopped. "Now," continued the headmaster, "I have some rather disturbing news for you. That flour bag woman, Mizz... your art

44

teacher, has been murdered on the school grounds..." he paused for gasps and muted cheers.... "Now, all of you who use striped red and black pencils, put up your hands." About a hundred hands went up. "Right, you lot remain in the hall; the rest of you..." he looked expectantly at the head boy who ordered a dismissal. The hall quickly emptied of all but the Staedtler pencil users. "O'Grady says 'sit!'" They sat. "Now, all of you whose pencils are HB, please stand!"

Most of the pupils looked uncertain - he didn't mention O'Grady - but a dozen of them promptly stood. "Right," said the headmaster, "you lot remain, the rest of you..." he looked expectantly at the head girl who ordered a dismissal. When the hall was cleared of all but the HB pencil users, the headmaster dismissed the staff. He stared balefully at the remaining pupils. They began to shuffle and fidget. There were seven girls and five boys. The youngest was eight years old, the oldest was twelve. "One of you," said the headmaster - his voice was almost a whisper - "is a murderer... or murderess. Are you going to confess, or do we have to wait this thing out?"

"It wasn't me," wailed the eight-year old, and she burst into tears. "Please, it wasn't me."

"We'll soon find out," said the headmaster. "Head boy and Head girl?"

"Sir?"

"Sir?"

"Search the bags of these suspects and let me know which is devoid of an HB pencil made by Staedtler. Do it!"

The two head prefects dashed to the foyer where pupils' bags were left during assembly, and thoroughly searched them. They soon returned, each carrying a bag, which they placed at the shoes of Mr Crakc. "No pencils in these bags, Sir," said the head boy.

"Right, will the owners of these bags come forward. The rest of you, "O'Grady says, dismiss!" Ten relieved children scuttled out of the hall. Two crestfallen children, including the weeping eight-year old, took up stooped positions next to their bags. The headmaster, the insides of his scrawny legs dripping molten ice, addressed the older of the two, a boy. "Can you explain why there is no pencil in your bag? I'm waiting."

"I was using it to play pencil cricket against Jones Minor, Sir, and it rolled into a crack in the floorboards."

"A likely story. You're a rugby player, aren't you?"

"Yessir. I'm in the first team. Hooker."

"Hooker, eh! I thought you were a boy."

"I am, Sir."

"Never mind. Just a joke. I put it to you that some time last night, on the rugby field, you murdered Mizz whatsisname by inserting a red and black striped pencil of Bosch manufacture into her... er..."

"No Sir, I didn't. I swear I didn't."

"Head girl, call Jones Minor. If he verifies your story, young Hooker, I'll let you go."

"Thank you, Sir."

The head girl dashed off to find the accused's alibi, and the headmaster turned to the little girl. "Little girl," he said, "where is your pencil?"

"I borrowed it to the aunty in the office, Sir," she whimpered.

"You *lent* it! Which Aunty? Mrs Jinks?"

"No Sir, Mrs Sidestitch. She was writing a story and her ball point ran out, so she asked if she could bo... lend my pencil."

"*Borrow*, child, *borrow*. And stop crying!"

"Sorry, Sir."

"So, the plot thickens. Mrs Sidestitch, eh?" The head girl appeared with Jones Minor in tow. He turned out to be a reliable alibi, which meant that there was only one remaining suspect: the bursar. Would she resist arrest? The headmaster decided that the head boy and the head girl should accompany him to the office.

His brindle complexion turned ashen when he saw the undead waiting for him at his door, waiting to apologise for missing assembly. She'd had to mend a tear in one of her flour bags. Why was Mrs Jinks

46

laughing at him? What was Mrs Sidestitch doing with the ... er... murder weapon in her hand?

"Mr Crack?" laughed Doris.

"It's 'Crakc' not 'Crack'!"

"Krak, then. I need your help. What's a word for 'appears to be real'?"

"Verisimilitude."

"Hang on... it fits but there's only three eyes. The clue says 'four eyes'".

"The fourth letter is an 'i', not a 'y', you blithering idiot!"

"You are the blithereen idiot, not me. You been makeen a total fool of yourself." She burst into renewed laughter and inserted the letters v,e,r,i,i,t,u,d to complete her crossword puzzle.

The headmaster's piles were throbbing painfully. "Why did you tell me that the flour bag woman had been murdered?"

"It's true - but only in Mrs Sidestitch's story what she wrote with a HB pencil, striped red and black. Stedla. She killed Mizz Reedbuck with a pencil, poison-tipped."

MASTER

When we found Roland Clarke dead in his armchair, one of the great mysteries of Ma'Nyoni's life was solved. She had been Roland's maid – I believe "domestic worker" is the more politically correct term – for nearly forty years, first in Gwanda, then in Plumtree, now in Bulawayo. She called him "Master", not because school mastering was his profession but as a synonym of "Duce" or "Fuehrer" or "Shogun".... Roland Clarke had been a History teacher. He had done time as Principal of a primary school in Gwanda, Head of Department at a secondary school in Plumtree, and, until his death, Deputy Headmaster of a secondary school in Bulawayo.

Roland Clarke MA had been a confirmed bachelor, terrified of the female sex, starting with his mother, Thalestris Q. Clarke PhD, one of whose less hyperbolic nicknames was Harridan of Hillside. Apparently she had forced her son to wear a bib at mealtimes well into his twenties. Miss Tweet, Head of English, had called him a misogynist and compared him with the eighteenth century British satirist, Alexander Pope, who once remarked: "Men, some to business, some to pleasure take, / But every woman is at heart a rake". The fact that Miss Tweet exemplified Pope's sentiments was neither here nor there. No one in the staff room allowed her to forget the time she was caught in her stock room with Metalwork; nor the time she was caught in the cricket pavilion with Management of Business; nor the time she was caught, precariously on the roof of the Music room with Design and Technology.

Roland was the epitome of neatness. The one thing he could not abide in a pupil was a shirt untucked. A boy caught bullying would be warned; a boy caught cheating would be threatened; but a boy caught with his shirt tail hanging out of his trousers would be beaten with a metre length of reinforced hosepipe. The Master's sartorial trim has been well documented in any number of school magazines, Speech Night eulogies, and PTA meetings. I recall a Newsletter, which went into rhapsodies over his footwear: strong outdoor shoes with wingtips and perforated toecaps, known to the initiated as Oxford brogues. He had worn them from the moment his feet had stopped growing at the age of sixteen – the number of times they had been re-soled over the years.

His jacket and trousers were tailor-made – no zips, damn you! – of a grey flannel material, famous for outlasting its wearer. His shirts, invariably white (off-white if the truth be told), with long sleeves and stiff (fraying if the truth be told) collars. His favourite tie sported the logo of his Alma Mater, the University of Rhodes, Grahamstown, South Africa, or "The Union", as Roland persisted in calling our southern neighbour. Nobody except, perhaps, maNyoni, could describe his underwear, but I imagined it to be loose and cottony.

The one thing MaNyoni could never understand about her obsessively neat and tidy employer was that he always left his wardrobe door open. It was almost the only work she had to do some days – close the wardrobe door. The dishes would be washed and put away, the floors would be swept, the furniture would be dusted, the garbage bin would be emptied, the pets would be fed. Roland Clarke, to the disgust of MaNyoni, loved pets, and he kept many of them: dogs, cats, birds, fish, and a miniature goat called Randolph who wreaked havoc in the home and the garden. He ate, banged, ate banged, from morn to dewy eve. He ate things that stood still like plants, clothes, and newspapers; and banged things that moved like dogs, cats, chickens, and MaNyoni's legs. Once, in an act that can only be described as rape, he mounted the moving back wheel of the Master's 1956 Austin Westminster.

The boys loved gruff old Mr Clarke. Once when he had to beat a junior for not pulling up his stockings on school premises, the blubbing child, after receiving two of the best, turned around and hugged him. Older boys invariably thanked him after receiving – not cuts, not with a piece of reinforced hosepipe, thwocks, rather – after receiving thwocks from the Deputy Headmaster. They liked him for his predictability, for his caricaturabilty; above all, for the fact that he genuinely liked them. He was even more popular than the recently graduated Physical Education teacher who allowed them to smoke during his lessons, and went drinking with them over the weekends. I too, was fond of the old fart, with all his old-fashioned ways. His presence made me feel unaccountably nostalgic. There was something of the ubi sunt about him – a vanished past.

When MaNyoni found him dead in his chair, she phoned the school. I happened to be free at the time, so I offered to go to his house and make the necessary arrangements. I found MaNyoni wringing her hands and muttering "Maye, bakithi!" over and over. She took me to his bedroom. He was slumped in his armchair, a barely sipped gin and tonic on a coaster on the side table. And there he was again, reflected in the full length mirror on the inside of his wardrobe door – slumped in his armchair, a barely sipped gin and tonic on a coaster, on the side table. "You see, MaNyoni," I said as I gently closed the wardrobe door, "we all need company, even the loneliest of us."

NGO GAMES

NGOs, like all of us, need time to unwind. They work under great pressure, and often in great danger, so utterly committed are they to the suffering masses of this earth. Once or twice a year it is the custom of those NGOs based in Sub-Saharan Africa to get together at some secluded venue, a safari lodge, say, and debrief(s) each other.

NGOs are a paradoxical lot. Among them you will find failed doctors, failed educators, failed lawyers, failed poets, failed priests, even. Yet as NGOs they are successes, precisely because they failed in their chosen careers. Jesus might have put it this way: "Those who fail will succeed; those who succeed will fail".

Success comes at a cost, however. These people are not too far from the front line when it comes to human rights issues. They avoid being beaten up or imprisoned if they can help it, but they compile reports, many reports, on those unfortunate souls who do get beaten up and imprisoned. Report writing is what NGOs do best, and report writing is one of the main events at the NGO Games. Other events include variety of sexual partners (not for the sake of sex but for commitment to tolerance and universalism), off-road driving skills, eating mopani worms and/or mice (to show solidarity with the suffering masses), video-watching marathon (of videos endorsed by Oxfam and Amnesty International – the last person to fall asleep wins), and an egg-and-spoon race.

At this year's games a number of countries was represented, countries which tended to have high unemployment rates at home, and which saw the NGO world as a respectable dumping ground for those

51

sons and daughters of theirs who couldn't face the stiff competition back home. Canada was there; Ireland was there; Germany was there; Denmark was there; Norway was there; Australia was there; South Africa was there; the Vatican City was there. Favourite for the "variety of sexual partners" category, this year, was Norway. This is not a racial thing, you understand. The concept of race, at least in biological terms, does not exist. The term is redundant. Genetically we are all the same (and not that much different from tomatoes); environmentally, however – and here colonization is largely to blame – we can be very different; hence the key word "variety" in this category. The countries represented had all done each other, but Norway had gone much further afield: Norway had done Swazi, Dinka, Hutu, Zezuru, Gikuyu, Hottentot, Berber, Pigmy, Maori, Easter Islander, and even – only once, mind you – Walloon.

As it turned out, Norway was beaten, edged out by relative newcomer, Vatican City; though Norway (good humouredly of course) cried foul at the fruits and vegetables on Vatican City's extensive list. The Off-road race was won by South Africa, only because favourite, Canada's vehicle had been painted maple leaf red. You see, a strict rule of this event is that all NGO vehicles (diesel fuelled Toyota 4 x 4s) must be painted white. Canada was disqualified. There was some consolation for Canada, however, which won the video-watching marathon, pushing the highly favoured Australia into second place. The first ten videos were on the plight of refugees all over the world; the second ten were on AIDS sufferers; the third ten were on North American prisons, the fourth on child soldiers, and the fifth... but nobody, not even Canada, got that far... was on female genital mutilation.

No one could match Germany in the report writing category. In the three days over which the course was run Germany produced no fewer than fourteen reports, all on the same topic, AIDS, and all pretty much repeat runs, but that is the nature of your NGO report. It's the tautological approach, where you say the same thing over and over again, but you say it differently. A typical NGO report would be structured in this way: first you say it in simple words, then you say it in difficult words, then you say it in words unfathomable to the layman, then you say it in pictures, then in maps, then in graphs, then in charts, then, and finally, in appendices.

The other countries cried foul (good humouredly, of course) when Ireland won the eating contest because Ireland, it turned out, was Zimbawe in the diaspora, and Zimbabwe rated among its delicacies, mice and mopani worms. And who won the egg and spoon race, the positive highlight of the games? Why, Denmark won it. So the only two countries not to take home a medal were Australia and Norway. But don't worry, they had a good time; they still are if that fuggy swaying 4 x 4, those Scandinavian shrieks and Antipodean groans are anything to go by.

OF THE FIST

"**L**et's go," growled Comrade Hondo shouldering his battered AK 47 and smashing his beer bottle against the wall of Mr Mutarara's store. Hondo was a genuine war veteran, now in his fifties. He was wearing a police uniform and had been given a temporary force number, and a temporary designation: Chief Warden. With him were seven youths designated by Joint Operations Command as Militias, and two brutalised farm workers. Their task that night, early morning if the glow on the eastern horizon was anything to go by, was to put into effect Operation Vote Wisely. They were armed with iron bars, the kind used to reinforce concrete. They were drunk.

Mr Mutarara's General Trading Store had been bought by his father in 1953, the year of the Centenary. It still displayed, somewhat anachronistically, faded advertisements for Aspro, Milk of Magnesia, and Rudge Cycles. It was a solidly built brick under corrugated iron structure and, except for a period during the Liberation Struggle when it had been regularly plundered by both sides in that bloody civil war, it had supplied the surrounding rural community, at a reasonable profit, with everything from mealie meal to wire nails.

No longer. When comrade Hondo and his group petrol bombed the store (the Mutarara family had already gone into hiding) they found nothing but three plastic coat hangers and two almost full crates of Castle lager. They had also been passing round a powerful distillation called, onomatopoeically, "tot-tot" accompanied by deep inhalations of the finest Gokwe *mbanje*, so by the time they left the fire-blackened shop they felt ready for anything.

"Anything" materialized into a seventy year old MDC activist called Mai Mwatse and her fourteen year old grand daughter, Chido. Their village, what was left of it, was located north of Harare in the Mazoe district, once famous for its oranges, still famous, somehow, for its orange juice. This was to be a mopping up operation; the real work had been done the night before. It had begun with an address by the MP elect for this constituency, retired Colonel Moscow Mhondi. In the middle of the night, villagers had been dragged from their huts and forced to assemble in the bush. The MP elect had harangued them for nearly three hours. The gist of his speech: if the country is given away through the ballot, we will go back to the bush and start another war. Then the villagers were forced to chant ZANU-PF slogans and sing *Chimurenga* songs. For hours. Then the beatings began. Then the killings. Limbs were broken, and backs (by laying the victims on a log, supine, see-saw style, and jumping on them); finally their heads were crushed. The MP elect broke many jaws with the butt of his rifle, and he presided over the killings, which were witnessed by the entire village including wives and children of the men who were killed.

The militias, also known as green bombers, wore T-shirts, combat jackets and trousers, and black boots. Their T-shirts portrayed the Esteemed Leader flapping his wrist at God, and the slogan: *tiri vechibhakera* (we are of the fist). The two brutalised farm workers wore rags. They were from retired Colonel Mhondi's farm. Douglas, the younger of the two, had been born on the farm, at the little clinic, which had been established by the previous owners, the Longbottoms. He had been schooled on the farm, and was in Grade Six when angry war veterans arrived in government vehicles without number plates and drove out the white owners and their labourers. Among those who ended up camping along roadsides, for months to come, were Douglas and his extended family.

One of those angry war veterans had been Comrade Hondo. Douglas remembered his demented eyes, red with battle-lust, as he set about killing the Longbottoms' pets. When the old, spayed Labrador bitch dared to challenge him, he grabbed it by the tail and swung it round several times before smashing its head against a wall of the farm house. The guinea pig and the budgie were easy. Only the cat got away.

Some of the children of the evicted labourers were allowed back to the farm where they underwent extensive re-education, which focussed on words like "revolution", "sovereignty", "colonialism", "imperialism", "racism"; and phrases like "puppet sanctions-mongers" and "Blair's kith and kin". Douglas had been one of these children, grateful for a daily plate of *sadza* and relish, which the farm no longer produced but which was freely available from Care International and other well-meaning suckers. When the harmonised elections of 11 March, 2008 went the wrong way, all retired Colonel Mhondi's farm workers (no longer labourers) were mobilised to help punish, with impunity, the misguided villagers throughout the country, but particularly in the previously ZANU PF strongholds, the three Mashonaland provinces.

Mai Mwatse and Chido had missed the previous night's *pungwe* because they had been in Harare to help care for the hundreds of displaced villagers who had taken refuge at Harvest House, the opposition headquarters. Mai Mwatse was a polling agent for her constituency and was, consequently, a marked person. When they got home the following day they were devastated to see that every single hut in the village, including their own, had been burned to the ground. The police had been and gone. Their task was to remove the bodies to the nearest mortuary, and those still alive but incapable of moving, to the nearest government hospital or clinic. They had strict instructions from the men at the top: Joint Operations Command: not to interfere with things political.

The traumatized community were huddled round an open fire - the nights were becoming chilly - when Comrade Hondo's party arrived. While his team stood guard on the outskirts of the circle of villagers, the war veteran went up to Mai Mwatse and ordered her to lie face down on the ground. "This is what we do to sell-outs," he growled, and he began beating her with an iron bar. Her screams excited the militia and one of the farm workers, and they joined in with the beating, all the while chanting: "Zimbabwe will never be a colony again!" Only Douglas, head lowered in shame, remained on the periphery.

Chido tried to protect her grandmother by throwing herself over the old woman's head. With a hobnailed boot Comrade Hondo nudged her onto her back and signalled to his *mujibas* to take her. The petrified crowd looked on. The farm worker was given the task of holding the girl down, by the shoulders; the dominant youth handed his iron bar to one of his subordinates, unbuckled his belt, and pulled his trousers down. Comrade Hondo wrenched Mai Mwatse's head in Chido's direction and forcefully held it there. Chido was sobbing, begging them to leave her alone. Two of the youths ripped off her underpants and pushed her dress above her navel. They forced her legs open and the dominant one went down on her. He humped her for so long that his comrades became impatient, called upon him to "release", "discharge", "unload". Finally the spasm came and he rolled off the whimpering child. The next one went down on her, and the next, and the next.... By the time the farm labourer took his turn, Chido was unconscious.

"This one is mine!" growled Comrade Hondo. He handed his iron bar to one of the militias, slipped his rifle off his shoulder, and barked an order to turn Mai Mwatse on her back. She was too broken from her beating to resist. "Hold open her legs! Whore of the white man! I am going to fuck your brains out!"

She gave a strangled cry as he rammed the barrel of his AK 47 into her vagina. "Do you know why this gun is called 47?" shouted Comrade Hondo. "Because it pumps 47 times before it comes. Count! COUNT!" He screamed at the audience, and they began to count. "Louder!" Forty Seven times he pushed the barrel in and out of the old woman's bloodied vagina. Then... "Let's come!" he laughed, and he fired three times into the woman's body.

On their way back to retired Colonel Mhondi's farm, which was being used as a torture centre, they mocked Douglas for being a coward, *mbwende*, and for behaving like a woman, *chikadzi*. Comrade Hondo went further and accused him of being a traitor, threatened to

57

kill him there and then. In a choked voice, Douglas said, "That old woman, she is my grandmother..."

"And that girl, that *musikana?*"

"Chido. She is my sister."

ORTHELLO

Dillard was taking his daily constitutional, a three kilometre round trip, which began at his front gate and ended at his back gate. It was a time for him to reflect on the unfairness of life and to prepare his work for the day. Looming large, at the moment, was his production of Shakespeare's *Othello,* the rehearsals for which had not been going too well. The performances were due in three days' time. His plan to cast a black Desdemona and a white Othello had been meeting with resistance. Logistically it made sense since only one white student (a male) had come for auditions; but it had created anomalies in the script, which still needed attending to.

It was Tuesday, which meant rubbish collection day for this part of Daleside. Dillard was shocked to see the number of scavengers around the bins, which were waiting to be emptied by the municipal garbage collectors; and the litter they scattered far and wide. The pied crows were worse than the humans who tended to be more selective in their choice of sweepings, rinsings and leavings. One old man with a ragged balaclava pulled over his face, in spite of the October weather, fished out a SPAR plastic bag, which had been tightly knotted. Dillard paused to watch him tear open the bag. Out fell a large dead rat. The old man picked it up by the tail and sniffed it before returning it to the metal dustbin. A small queue had formed behind the old man, mainly of primary school children in their ill-fitting hand-me-downs. A Lucky Dip queue!

Even at this time of the morning the heat was oppressive, though the jacaranda blossoms did not seem to mind; and Dillard could not recall a time when the bougain villaea vines had looked so splendid;

such a variety of brilliant colour; such vicious thorns, mind you! Already the sprinklers were going. He could hear them behind the two metre instarect walls topped with razor or electric wire. It was the garbage bins from these houses that were attracting crows, stray dogs and Bulawayo's rapidly growing tribe of human offscourings.

Ahead of him to the left, a sleek electronically controlled gate opened for an equally sleek Mercedes Benz driven by a not so sleek representative of Bulawayo's *nouveau riche*. Dillard recognized Desdemona's father and gave him a coy greeting, which was returned with bluster. A stanza from one of this year's A-Level poems swam into his consciousness:

'The city filled with orange trees
is lost', which, interpreted, meant
all conspicuous luxuries
augur ruinous punishment.

Not that many orange trees left in Bulawayo. Not that many *makiwas* either. Plenty of jacarandas, though; and silver oaks, and flamboyants, and eucalyptus. Botanical colonization was proving more resilient than its human equivalent. Dillard was one of only three white teachers left at his school, all middle-aged or elderly. The best black and brown teachers had also left for greener pastures – not that you're going to find too much green pasture in Francistown or Pietersburg or Darwin.

Five years ago there hadn't been a single vendor on his route; now he counted thirty: ten for each kilometre. All the vendors were either women or children. They created little tables out of cardboard boxes or bits of paving. On these surfaces they displayed, ever so neatly, their meagre stock: overripe tomatoes and bananas, cigarettes (sold individually), boiled sweets, and the ubiquitous "penny cools". As a consequence of these vendors and their miniature tuck-shops, Dillard's route had become fouled with tons of litter, dominated by the transparent plastic "penny cool" containers.

At first Dillard thought that the vendors worked for themselves until he began to notice a Pajero with tinted windows, which visited each site periodically. He made a few discreet enquiries and was not that surprised to learn that a single entrepreneur, very well connected in ruling party circles, owned all these tuckshops, and many more besides. Dillard learnt, furthermore, that there was a tuckshop war going on in the suburbs of Bulawayo. The tinted Pajero had held a monopoly until the BMW with blackened windows sidled into view.

Nowadays Dillard had to make several detours from his regular route since there were so many leaks from the municipal water system. Spreckley Road resembled a Venetian canal, while it would soon be possible to go white water rafting down William Shakespeare Avenue. As recently as a few months back, the municipality would have responded promptly to a reported leak; now they didn't even answer the phone. It had not taken the ruling party long to bankrupt Bulawayo, an MDC stronghold. The city of Kings was dying.

One of his detours took Dillard past the palatial residence of Othello's family. He heard the sprinklers going, and from the house a famous Country and Western singer whose name Dillard couldn't remember but whose tits and mop of bottle blonde hair he could clearly visualise, was belting out a song with the refrain: "Nine to five". Their rubbish bin was being besieged by no fewer than five scrawny school children. Behind the electric gate a boerbul and a rotweiler, in a frenzy to get at the children, were attacking each other. A beautifully

61

lettered sign on the wall near the gate read: IF YOU ENTER THESE PREMISES WITHOUT PERMISSION YOU WILL BE EATEN ALIVE.

The Othello family were also part of Bulawayo's ostentatious *nouveau riche*. Upstarts, Dillard like to call them. Dillard came from pioneer stock. His great grandfather had been an Anglican missionary in the Inyati area. His grandmother had been born in old Mangwe Fort during the 1896 Matabele rebellion. He could go on! Othello's father had made his fortune in the early years of Independence, in what is euphemistically termed "buying and selling". All you needed was one corrupt senior civil servant, preferably attached to Customs and Immigration. Desdemona's father had to wait a little longer, when unbudgeted payouts to war veterans, forays into the DRC, and the agricultural reform programme (also known as the Third Chimurenga) created a black market economy where black, white, and brown marketeers became shockingly rich in a shockingly short period of time, while the rest of the country grew abject. Desdemona's father "bought" food donated by various NGOs, repackaged it, and sold it to the rural poor. He also dabbled in diesel, paraffin, and cooking oil.

What to do about the play! How could you have a white Othello when the text called for a Moor, "thick-lips", an "old black ram"? How could you have a black Desdemona when the text called for a Venetian, "that whiter skin of hers than snow", a "white ewe"? Simple: change the text; update it; localise it. That's what you do to Shakespeare. How about "thin-lips"? How about "an old white ram is tupping your black ewe"? How about "that blacker skin of hers than coal"? No, not "coal": that's racist. "Ebony"? Yes, that's better. Hang on! Ebony's a heavy, dark wood used for making furniture. Does it really have positive connotations? "That blacker skin of hers, than ebony". Not so sure. Besides it's not iambic. Got to be a single syllable. "Jet"? Possibly, but it's still a type of coal! "Sable"? Sad and un-iambic. Not so simple after all.

Then Dillard had a flash of inspiration. Change Moor to Zimbabwean, Venetian to Rhodesian (goodness, it almost rhymed!)- the rest would fall into place. Hang on a moment! Then the only white actor in the play would be Zimbabwean, and all the other actors, all black or brown, would be Rhodesians! Try it the other way round: change Moor to Rhodesian, Venetian to Zimbabwean. Let's test it: what does Brabantio say?

> Look to her, Moor, if thou hast eyes to see:
> She has deceived her father and may thee.

Okay:

> Look to her, Rhodesian...

No, that buggers up the metre. What about:

> Look, Rhodesian, if thou hast eyes to see:
> She has deceived her father and may thee.

Not bad, but what about when Shakespeare speaks metaphorically? When the Duke tries to console Desdemona's father, doesn't he say something like, "And noble signior"... something like:

> If virtue no delighted beauty lack,
> Your son-in-law is far more fair than black.

Now the problem isn't metre, it's rhyme. If I change it to "far more black than fair", I'm going to have to find a word to rhyme with "fair". Let's see…er…what about:

> If virtue's qualities are always rare
> Your son-in-law is far more black than fair.

Bit clumsy. What if I change "fair" to "white"? Um…what about:

> If virtue lack no beauties that delight
> Your son-in-law is far more black than white.

Better: "white" has fewer positive connotations than "fair". Needs more work, though. Certainly needs more work.

Dillard was looking forward to a pot of tea and a couple of slices of toast when he unlatched his back gate. And he must phone the printers to see if the *Othello* programme was ready. But there was a power failure, and the phone lines were down. Then he noticed that he had been burgled. Gone was his digital radio (never to be replaced); gone was his Toshiba laptop (never to be replaced); gone was his unopened bottle of Green Valley wine (likely to be replaced).

Worse was yet to come. When he arrived at school – late again, Mr Dillard! - the office informed him that his programmes had been delivered by the printers. He tore open the package, thumbed out a programme, only to find that they had mispelt the title, and that he was going to produce a play called *Orthello*.

PROFILE OF A SCHOOL TEACHER

Mr Abednego Dolobeni owned two Emergency Taxis (or ETs), which plied the routes from Eleventh Avenue, out along the Khami road to Mpopoma; and Twelfth Avenue extension, out along the Old Esigodini Road to Hotel Rio. His taxis were Volkswagen Kombis with Peugeot 404 engines. Originally seven-seaters, he had converted them into sixteen-seaters, eighteen at a push.

The income generated from this enterprise helped Mr Dolobeni re-stock his two farms: one a mere 300 acres in the Bulilila communal lands, which he had taken over from his older (now late) brother; the other a once thriving dairy farm near Falcon College in Esigodini, which the government had taken from the owners because they were white and had been in Africa for only four generations. He had qualified for the farm because he was an ex-combatant, having spent six weeks in a training camp in Tanzania, where he nearly died of sleeping sickness. He re-stocked the communal farm with down-market bottle stores, and the dairy farm with down-market motels.

The income generated from this enterprise helped Mr Dolobeni send his two daughters, Roberta and Gabriella, to a private school in England where they grew sleek on Mars bars and rice pudding. It also helped him finance the never-ending university courses he studied for in the only free time available to him – his mornings at Umgababa Secondary School where he taught Bible Studies and Business Management. He used the time in his Bible Study lessons to pursue an M.B.A. through the University of South Africa, and the time in his Business Management lessons to complete his Masters in Education through the Open University in Zimbabwe. He also managed to

65

persuade one of the senior pupils, a prefect, to preside over his extra-mural activities, which included soccer coaching and Scripture Union.

Mr Dolobeni was a member of ZIMTA (the Zimbabwe Teachers Association) and an A-level examiner in Management of Business. He was, in fact, the Chief Examiner in this subject, a position he thoroughly deserved since most of his students at Umgababa Secondary School achieved A or B grades, and none ever failed.

Everybody knows how badly teachers are paid so no one begrudged Mr Dolobeni his private lessons with innumerable students from his own and other schools. His fee was reasonable, and he taught in his classroom, after hours, over the weekends, and during the school holidays. No wonder his Headmaster assessed Mr Dolobeni five out of five, year after year.

He was an immaculate dresser thanks to accounts at, among other stores, Edgars, Truworths, The Shirt Man, and Athlete's World. He had a different pair of shoes for every day of the week, and the best were made of elephant hide. His ties were stunning – made of pure silk, and imported from Italy; bright as butterflies. He had seven sports jackets, fourteen pairs of trousers and four three-piece suits. On extra special occasions, like Speech Day, he wore white gloves. But the apparel he was famous for – as far south as Gwanda, and as far north as Gweru – were his shirts. Break your heart, Mandela!

There is something else you need to know about Abednego Dolobeni [not his real name]; he is a member of the C.I.O. (Central Intelligence Organization), and he is responsible for the exclusion, transfer, even disappearance, of a number of his erstwhile colleagues – upstarts who dared to criticize the man whose portrait hangs in every school hall in the entire country.

Let this brief profile of a school teacher be a lesson to those who call us "men among schoolboys and schoolboys among men"; who quote: "Those who can, do; those who can't, teach"; who claim that we don't deserve a pay increase because we have such a light work load and so many holidays. Let this, I repeat, be a lesson.

QUITE EPIPHANIC, REALLY.

Licking walls and chewing coal were not the only cravings glorious Gloria developed when she became pregnant for the first time. She discovered the art of bonsai, which appealed to her *elan vital*. In the ornamental miniature tree she perceived not the flesh and bones, not the word, but the… well… a kind of pervasive transforming influence, like leaven. How did whatshisname put it:

> Full fathom five thy father lies;
> Of his bones are coral made:
> Those are pearls that were his eyes:
> Nothing of him that doth fade,
> But doth suffer a sea-change
> Into something rich and strange.

Yes. A merging of nature and art. Not bones and eyes; not poetry; but coral and pearls – *bon* and *sai*. Quite epiphanic, really.

Glorious Gloria's husband, Anthinny, was one of those Chartered Accountants who did not fantasize about being a lion tamer; consequently he, his suburban utility vehicle, and his complete set of Gary Player golf clubs were a calming influence on the mother-to-be. He looked upon her eccentric behaviour with amused tolerance, and lavished her and the embryo with gifts inclining to the colour blue. While at school Anthinny had played first team rugby, and he was determined to repeat that transcendent experience, vicariously, through his son, er… they hadn't yet thought of a name. Something Biblical, perhaps, like Mawk, or Mathew. But what if it's a girl? Darn it, life's complicated!

Gloria started looking round for specimens, and hit the jackpot at a nursery on the Old Esigodini road, which had gone bankrupt and was selling its stock at giveaway prices. Among that stock were a number of indigenous trees, which had been unsold for years; consequently they had become root-bound in their black plastic containers, and already looked a bit like bonsais. She chose a baobab, a pod mahogany and, unfortunately it seems, a rain tree. Then she went looking for containers: a deep flared oval for the pod mahogany, a rectangle with lip (soft corners) for the baobab, and a round cascade for the fateful rain tree. She bought some potting soil, some horticultural grit, and some composted bark. She already had the basic tools: a small pair of scissors for cutting shoots, a pair of tweezers for picking off bugs, secateurs for pruning and cutting roots, and a chopstick (nice touch) for combing out roots.

As the baobab was already teetering to one side, she decided (nibbling a piece of coal) to shape it in the *Windswept* or Fukinagashi style. The *Literati* or Bunjin style would suit the erect pod mahogany, while the rain tree, already seriously stressed, would be made more visually exciting with a bit of deadwood, a *jin*, to the better informed.

First things first. The specimens had to be transferred from their battered black plastic sleeves to the new stoneware containers. This required some quite ruthless snipping and combing of roots (quick lick of the dining room wall). Gloria asked her domestic worker, Eatmore, to help her, and that was when the trouble began. Eatmore took one look at the savaged rain tree and ran screaming out of the house.

A sugared bun never failed on occasions like these, and once Eatmore was back in the house, Gloria asked her why the panic.

69

Eatmore came from a tribe, which regarded the rain tree with great suspicion. She called it *ichithamuzi*. Water dripped from its leaves before the onset of the seasonal rains. Families who used its wood to make fire were destroyed. She urged Gloria to return it to the nursery, but Gloria dismissed Eatmore's fear with amused contempt (these people!), and gave her another sugared bun.

Gloria then got to work. She (well, Eatmore) washed the pots and covered the drainage holes with plastic mesh. She showed Eatmore how to insert the anchorage wire through one hole and back up another, and then how to spread the soil mixture across the base of the pot. Gloria did not trust the girl with secateurs so she herself had to cut back the sapling's fibrous roots, shorten heavy roots, and create a compact root system at the trunk base. It made her feel quite sexy, somehow.

When it came to planting, Eatmore refused to handle the rain tree. Gloria called her a stupid *into* and sent her off to scrub floors. Single-handed now, glorious Gloria positioned each tree on the soil to give the correct front view. Then she brought the anchorage wires across each rootball [am I boring you?], and twisted them together. Once she felt that the trees were secure, she added more soil and gently worked it into the root masses until the containers were full. Then she watered them well. Later she would decorate the surfaces with moist moss.

In order to create more attractive silhouettes, she adjusted the trunks and some of the branches of the trees with pliable copper wire. But she wasn't yet finished with the rain tree - what did Eatmore call it? eekeetamooshi, or something. Honestly, these people! A *jin* gives the impression of age. It makes the tree look as if it has been naturally damaged. Now, unnaturally, Gloria damaged the rain tree. She tore off a good third of its bark, leaving the white wood underneath exposed.

Proudly she displayed her three bonsais on a table in a sunny corner of the lounge, and received many sighs and gasps of admiration from her friends, all pretty and all married to Chartered Accountants who had no intentions of switching to lion taming.

The pod mahogany flourished, the baobab flourished, but the rain tree, never healthy in captivity, sickened and died. Eatmore refused to touch it so Gloria, now heavily pregnant, had to do it. Sadly she removed *lonchocarpus capassa* from the round cascade pot and threw it into the fire place. By now she'd lost interest in the art of bonsai so the rain tree's replacement was a pink geranium. Ah, cute, man!

Anthinny was present at the birth. It was a terrible labour. Hours and hours. The baby's head was huge. He watched it crowning. Before he could be absolutely sure he cried out: "It's a…er…and then he fell silent. The paediatrician took over: "It's a… er…person of restricted growth; quite epiphanic, really."

ROSEWATER

He was not exactly camp, not visually anyway; but he saturated himself with the sweet scent of roses, a scent that remained in the classroom even when he wasn't there. I didn't mind; in fact I rather enjoyed it; it seemed to have a calming effect on the more rowdy boys. His nickname was Rosewater.

I had known he was gay. In the third term of his second year at school he had written me a deeply embarrassing composition entitled "To Sir with Love". I doubt if anyone else beyond his intimate friends knew, since, in his culture, homosexuality was taboo. It was a colonial thing, a white thing; it was unAfrican. There certainly wasn't anything effeminate about the way he threw a discus or put a shot. And, while he permeated scrum after scrum, ruck after ruck, maul after maul, with attar of roses, it was not thurification which won him, two years running, full colours for rugby in a rugby-obsessed school. He looked macho, behaved macho, talked macho... but he smelled of Rosa damascena.

He carried it around with him in a plastic atomiser, the kind gardeners use to spray insecticide on plants. He used it sparingly in cooler weather, but when it was hot - and it is hot most of the time in this part of the world - he sprayed it all over him and all round him. Our incense-bearer.

It happened when Rosewater was in his final year at high school. He was a senior prefect and captain of the athletics team; he was one of the school's best academics. I'll never forget that night as long as I live, and I'll never know what, finally, pushed him to do it. Later, much later, come to think of it, I was reminded of Auden's lines:

About suffering they were never wrong,
the Old Masters: how well they understood
its human position; how it takes place
while someone else is eating or opening a window or just walking
dully along.

How art informs life! I was probably doing one of those mindless things when it took place. Forty years now, a man among schoolboys, a lower case old master; eating the leftover wing of a chicken filched from the cook matron's pantry; or opening the window of my single room in the hostel to let in a fresh supply of sewage-and-deodorant, socks-and-chlorine, floor polish-and-orange peel scented air: the redolence of boarding school; or, yes, just walking dully along.

Why not me? Why this aromatic golden boy?

I happened to be on duty. There came a breathless banging on my door. Two or three juniors, whimpering like puppies. Sir, Sir! Come quick! It's Rosewater. He's dead! In the bath! He's dead, Sir! Please, Sir, come quick! It's "quickly", not "quick"! Don't you know the difference between an adjective and an adverb? What do you mean he is dead? If this is one of your sick jokes.... No joke, Sir. It's true. Please....

When I found that he was indeed dead in the bath, as I groped for the slightest sign of life, the jugular, the carotid, the mutilated wrists; and as I too began whimpering like the juniors cowering behind me, I was struck by something almost numinous. The characteristic smell of Rosewater had metamorphosed into a sight incarnadine, which gurgled away as I pulled the rubber plug.

SEWERAGE PIPE

Shorn Coleridge had decided to commit suicide, or "sewerage pipe", as he jokingly called it. He was going to do something predictable like hanging or poison. A bullet in the mouth, pointing brainwards, required too much red tape, too much economic outlay. Jesus, guns were expensive. He went to the local hardware store and bought three metres of sash cord, and a box of Ratkill. He took these items home and put them next to each other on the dining room table. How to decide. He thought of going "eeny meeny miny mo..." but that meant he would have to use the racist word, "nigger"; so he searched the house for a coin to toss. Easier said than done. Coins had been out of circulation for months in Zimbabwe. Only the brown, $20 000 Bearer cheques were of any value: about six potatoes of value. He found no coin, but during the search an idea came to him. Why not die usefully?

The government, which had been in power since independence in 1980, looked as if it was going to remain in power for ever – unless the suffering masses took to the streets in their tens of thousands, in their hundreds of thousands (leave millions, billions, and trillions to the fiscus) and protested. Protested against vote rigging, politicisation of the police and the armed forces, the judiciary, the church, chiefs, domestic pets even. Shorn still bore the scars on his left index finger of the chomp of an African Grey; and his friend Shawn de Quincey still limped from the time a Rhodesian Ridgeback had buried its fangs in the region of his sciatic nerve.

Yes, why not die usefully? Why not initiate a mass protest right here in Bulawayo. The town was already teeming with the unemployed, and with school children whose parents could no longer afford the

74

fees. He needed a banner and a loud hailer. He would set himself up at the City Hall, under the clock; and then once enough of a crowd had gathered, he would lead them along Sel... er... Leopold Takawira Avenue towards the Law Courts. There would be bloodshed, and Shorn would be a prime target, but by the time he fell, still clutching his banner, the protesters would be so numerous that the police would take to their heels. News of the uprising would quickly spread to Harare, thence to Masvingo, Mutare, Gweru, Kwekwe, maybe even Colleen Bawn. The masses would rise up, and the government would fall.

He made a banner out of a single-bed white sheet and two broom handles. Using thick, felt tipped pens, blue, red, and green, he wrote: DOWN WITH THE GOVERNMENT. DOWN WITH ZANU-PF POOFTAS. He used drawing pins to connect the sheet to the broom handles, rolled it carefully as if it were some sacred scroll, and carried it over his shoulder to town. (He couldn't get hold of a loud hailer.)

He chose a week day when the streets and pavements of Bulawayo were at their most crowded. He recognized the uniforms of at least twelve schools, primary as well as secondary. The unemployed, surprisingly well dressed thanks to unscrupulous credit facilities at clothing stores, which plunged them into irrecoverable debt, wandered aimlessly about or hovered near news stands in the hope of getting a free read of the Chronicle, or last week's Independent, or the previous week's Standard, or the week prior to that['s] Johannesburg Sunday Times. Beggars there were, and street kids aplenty: rivals, for junk food scraps, of pied crows, sparrows, pigeons, and *Rattus rattus alexandrinus*.

The banner unfurled was too wide to hold in his hands so he persuaded a couple of street children to hold it for him. Then he began to hurl philippics. People gathered, pointed, smiled, laughed, clicked their tongues. The street children soon grew tired of their task and allowed the banner to tilt. One of them squatted, which created a hypotenuse effect. Not much of the banner remained legible.

Enough, however, for a pack of teenage militias, recent graduates from one of the Border Gezi training camps, who had been taught that any kith and kin of Blair and his gay gangsters, was Zimbabwe's enemy number one. There were three girls and six boys, identically dressed in green combat outfits, black boots, black belts, and black batons.

As they converged on Shorn, the small crowd he had attracted quickly dispersed to a safe distance from where they could watch the action. The street kids dropped the banner and took to their heels. Down came the batons, in went the boots; and as consciousness began to fade from Shorn's mind he regretted only that his death wouldn't, hadn't, achieve[d] anything useful. He was vaguely aware of screaming, as one of the broom handles rammed into his bottom, or "sewerage pipe", as the militias jokingly called it.

SNOWMAN

The night before our departure we had dinner with the Afrikaans teacher, Miss Devine. She was a seasoned traveller; she had some good tips for us. "Take long johns with you," she said, "and never accept a drink that has already been poured from the bottle. You never know what they might have laced it with." She exploited the feature of definiteness in the fricative "they", held it for a longer period than usual between her tongue and her dentures. The pressure slightly dislodged the latter, producing a whistling sound as of kettles boiling.

"More pumpkin, boys?" We politely declined a third helping of the sweet orange pulp flavoured with nutmeg. We wanted to keep some space for dessert, Miss Devine's speciality: pumpkin fritters rolled in sugar and cinnamon. The Afrikaans teacher was no pushover when it came to pumpkin recipes. Her jaundiced complexion was a result, not of an obstructed bile duct or of some liver disease like hepatitus, but by the regular consumption of enormous quantities of pumpkin.

"How are your drinks? Let me banish the daylight from your glasses." This joke was not weakened by the fact that it was late in the evening, the crepuscular time when *eros* and *thanatos* merge in the imagery of light and shade… even though the Christmas beetles had not gone to bed, and at least one Heuglin's robin was concurring with Miss Devine's admonition to "take warm things…take warm things…take warm things…" We gladly offered our glasses for a refill. There was no denying the potency of Miss Devine's home-made peach brandy, which she called *mampoer,* and which gave her nose a reddish glow. This, combined with her cupreous cheeks, reminded many of her admiring pupils past and present of the warm end of the visible spectrum.

"And another thing, boys - if you ever get the urge to spend a penny out in the open, do it through a sock. Otherwise your *dinguses* [things] will snap off. I tell you, it's going to be cold enough to freeze the brass off a bald monkey. Isn't that how the English expression goes?" We thought it did. "Dress warm boys; which reminds me; I've got something for you." She bustled off down the passage while we sipped away at the liquid lightning in our glasses; which was reciprocated by a real bolt from the sky. It, briefly, restored the daylight Miss Devine had so hubristically banished. A stifling, pre-storm lull was seeping into our necks and armpits.

The Afrikaans teacher returned with gifts for each of us: body belts made from two of her old bras, and knitted tea cosies, brown and yellow for me, blue and red for my friend. Both sported green pompons, so large that they tilted to one side. We were to wear them on our heads, day and night because "As long as your head is warm, you will survive the bitter European winter. Janee - *'n warm kop, 'n warm dop, en julle sal deurkom."* [yes no – a warm head, a warm shot, and you'll make it]

Our Rhodesian education had fully prepared us to sample the cultural delights of Europe: we wanted to get hold of as much pornography as possible and, in a more sentimental vein, we wanted to visit the real Kensington gardens where our favourite literary character, Peter Pan had been conceived. We dreamed of the Broad Walk, the Round Pond, rhododendrons, and the River Serpentine. But we dreamed even more of pussy, nay, we were obsessed by it.

"So, what do you boys intend seeing while you are in Europe? I muttered something about the Popadopoulis, and my friend thought

78

we might visit the Eiffel Flats. The seasoned traveller, Miss Devine, gently corrected us. She then went on to recommend Delville Wood in Belgium where two of her uncles had perished in the First World War, the Rhodesian Ridgeback Society in Vienna, and the statue of Jannie Smuts in London.

Neither of us had experienced snow, except for the stuff you see in a deep freeze, which doesn't really count; and the balls of cotton wool on our Christmas trees, which also doesn't really count. There was, of course, no shortage of literary snow in our colonial education, driven, flurried, and flaked by conscientious expatriate teachers. There were the "snows of yesteryear"; there was the cherry, "hung with white upon the bough"; there was Mary's little lamb "whose fleece was white as snow"; and, in the bleak mid-winter of Christina Rossetti's bitter imagination there was "snow on snow, / snow on snow". My friend was particularly excited about building a snowman with a carrot for a nose and two pieces of coal for eyes. You could almost hear him thinking where the blue and red tea cosy with a green pompon would end up. Miss Devine called him Frosty, and the name stuck.

I was gagging on my third pumpkin fritter when the lightning grew more intense, and the thunder: five, then four, then three, then two counts away. Down came the rain, up wafted the scent of Africa: sweetening dust. The temperature around the dining room table immediately cooled, and we all cheered the glorious downpour. Before departing we helped the Afrikaans teacher put pots, pans, enamel basins, and other assorted containers underneath the many places where her house leaked; helped shut windows; helped comfort terrified pets; helped the old lady on with her much travelled raincoat, which she liked to call a mackintosh, since she had purchased it many years before in Scotland, birthplace of Andrew Murray, founder of her beloved Dutch Reformed Church.

With a *"Lekker ry,* [pleasant journey] my billy boys," Miss Devine, the retired Afrikaans teacher, now in her eighties, kissed and hugged us goodbye. She had accompanied us all the way to the gate. We promised to send her a post card from each of our destinations, our first, and as it turned out, our last, being Zurich, Switzerland.

*   *   *

Looking, I guess, ridiculous in our tea cosies and our Matabeleland rugby jerseys, Frosty and I eventually arrived (it was late evening) in Zurich, Switzerland. We were indeed stunned by the cold, so cold that there was more ice than snow on the ground. It made us gasp. When we left Bulawayo Airport, waved all the way into the sky by our loving moms and dads and brothers and sisters, the temperature had been squatting in the shade at 37 degrees centigrade. Here it was minus 20 degrees centigrade. Our *dinguses* virtually disappeared. Frosty would get to build his snowman.

We found a cheap downtown hotel, on the advice of *Europe on Ten Dollars a Day,* and soon settled in, although the oompah band downstairs was pretty hair raising, and we were shocked at the price of food and drink. What little money we had, we decided, would be spent on our main reason for taking this trip: sex. The real thing, while preferable to pornography, was a little too daunting for us at this stage, though we could not take our eyes off the oompah groupies. Not far from the hotel was a flea pit of a cinema, which advertised a double-bill. We had little Afrikaans and less German but we could get the gist of the titles: *Ich bin ein Nymphomaniac* and *Mädchen mit öffnen Lippe*. Besides there was nothing ambiguous about the accompanying stills.

On the way to the cinema we passed a small shop which advertised bananas at what seemed to be a reasonable price. We decided that we should eat something since the double billing was likely to prove a marathon. I could count to ten in German and I knew how to say "please" but I was darned if I knew the word for bananas. Perhaps it was the same as the Afrikaans, *piesang*". I persuaded Frosty to go in and make the order, while I waited outside. I was a real coward. I said, "Just say, '*Zwei piesangs, bitte?*' and point to the bananas. I watched Frosty through the shop window. He approached a burly viking of a woman, said the words and pointed to the bananas. She didn't seem to understand him, and I watched him repeat the words. Suddenly she gave him such a bang on the side of his head that his tea cosy fell off. When she started making Teutonic screams we ran for it.

"What was that all about?" I asked Frosty once I'd managed to get my breath back in the freezing cold of the street. He didn't know. He thought it may have been the Afrikaans word, which she might have taken as an insult. He grumbled at me for getting him into that fix.

The first film was *Mädchen mit geöffneten Lippne*. We gasped, but not with cold. It was during a particularly sizzling scene, which involved among other curious items, a gigantic syringe, that Frosty fainted against my side. I managed to revive him but he said he could no longer watch the movie. He would wait for me outside. I should have gone out with him and taken him to the hotel but I was desperate to see the movie through.

I barely gave Frosty a thought when I decided to watch the second feature, which began after a ten minute interval. My throat was dry with lust, and I had a banana of an erection. A woman official with a discreet torch walked up and down the rows of seats to make sure that there was no hanky panky going on. She had already thrown out an elderly man in a trench coat.

Then there was an unscheduled, free, third feature. I couldn't believe my good fortune. It was called *Der Teufel in Fräulein Divine*, and it featured a hollowed out pumpkin! O the long arm of coincidence! I half expected to see the ochreous Afrikaans teacher in a supporting role. The previous two films would have been classified as soft porn; this was the real thing *[dingus]*. This wasn't maids, turned bottles, calling aloud for corks; this was maids well and truly corked. Meanwhile, the woman official with the transferred epithet in her hand was kept busy evicting transgressors in what Miss Devine would have called mackintoshes.

It was only after this bonus third feature had ended and I had taken a few minutes for subsidence to occur, that I remembered Frosty. He would have gone back to the hotel. Surely? I found him on the pavement outside the cinema, in a sitting position, covered in snow. His tea cosy was slightly awry. His eyes were black, like shiny pieces of coal, and his nose had taken on the brittle texture of a carrot. Coins were strewn about him. I counted thirty. Frosty was frozen stiff; quite dead.

TAKING THE WATERS

I was drawn to the second hot pool of this Namibian spa by the amazing sight of Amarylis Leghorn positioning herself so that a massage jet designed to reach the lower back, reached, with some measure of success if the beatific expression on her face was anything to go by, the lower front. I eased myself into the soothing water until it gently lapped my throat then I crab-walked to within earshot of two men who were simultaneously massaging their insteps and arguing about religion. One of these men was Bouncer Leghorn; the other turned out to be some sort of a preacher, who commuted between Margate, Natal, and Perth, Australia. Name of Moral MacBraggert. His breath, as it drifted across the sulphurous waters, smelled of violets.

They were arguing about sacrifice, it seemed: Bouncer, a promising career as a cricketer, for marriage to Amarylis; Moral, Mammon for God. Bouncer wanted to know why Moral had made such a sacrifice if he didn't have to, whereas Moral commended Bouncer for his sacrifice. I tuned in at a point where Moral was justifying his sacrifice with scripture: "No one can serve two masters. Either he will hate the one and love the other, or he will be devoted to the one and despise the other. You cannot serve both God and money." Matthew 6, verse 24. It's in Luke too."

Bouncer was incredulous: "But surely you don't take Jesus at his word?"

"I surely do take Jesus at his word. Jesus IS the word." He smiled pityingly at Bouncer while his left foot changed places with his right foot, on the water jet, training it against his instep.

83

"So when he tells you to love your enemy as yourself you obey him?"

"I surely do, my friend."

Amarylis, straddling the lower back jet, a little way from us, suddenly, and with no apparent reason, half called, half gasped: "Oh my God, yes!" Which Moral seemed to take as a confirmation of his avowal but which Bouncer pretended not to notice.

"And when he says you can't be his disciple unless you hate your family -"

"Jesus doesn't say that."

"Oh God, no. Oh God, no."

"He bloodywell does! And if you're a preacher, you're one of his personal followers..."

"I am, praise the Lord!"

"Oh... oh...oh...!"

"So? Do you hate your family?"

"Of course I don't hate my family. The family is the most important thing on earth. It is central to Christianity. The family is -"

"Where does Jesus say that?"

"Say what?"

"Oh God, yes. Oh God, yes."

"All that crap about the family."

"...Er... `Honour thy father and thy mother'."

I couldn't resist coming in at this point. I'm a great admirer of Jesus even though I don't for a minute believe that he was divine. Without so much as an introduction, I said (taking unfair advantage by consulting the Bible that is lying open on my desk) I said: "Jesus might quote that commandment more than once, but he himself contradicts it more than once. For instance, in Matthew, 10, verse 35, he says: `For I am come to set a man at variance against his father, and the daughter against her mother...'; and in Matthew, 8, verses 21 and 22: And another of his disciples said unto him, Lord suffer me first to go and bury my father. But Jesus said unto him, Follow me; and let the dead bury their dead'; and in Luke,11, verses 27 and 28: And it came to pass, as he spake these things, a certain woman of the company lifted up her voice, and said unto him, Blessed is the womb that bare thee, and the paps which thou hast sucked. But he said, yea rather, blessed are they that hear the word of God, and keep it'. I could go on: when Jesus was just twelve years old his parents lost him for three days! Sick with worry, they eventually found him sitting in a temple in Jerusalem discussing theology with the elders. When his mother said to him: `Son, why hast thou thus dealt with us? Behold, thy father and I have sought thee sorrowing', Jesus, without the slightest remorse or consideration, replies: `How is it that ye sought me? Wist ye not that I must be about my father's business?' Jesus' mother seems to have been dead scared of him. In John, 2, we read of a marriage in Cana to which both Jesus (with his disciples tagging along) and his mother are invited. There is no wine, it seems, so Mary, with some trepidation, goes to her son and says: 'They have no wine'.

Jesus replies: "Woman, what have I to do with thee? Mine hour is not yet come.'

Mary urges the servants: `Whatsoever he saith unto you, do it.'

Jesus does not honour his mother and his father; and he doesn't seem to be the slightest bit interested in the family as an institution. I'm inclined to agree with you, Mr...er...?"

"Leghorn. John Leghorn. My friends call me Bouncer."

I introduced myself and we shook wet hands. Then I turned to the preacher. All the while I had spoken he had kept a smile and had gazed upon me with pitying eyes, a baby blue colour, reflecting the stinking waters of the pool.

Bouncer spoke next, with one eye on his wife who had left the pool and was lying peacefully on one of those low, padded, reclining seats which you always find at spas. "You say you love your enemy; that's a difficult one to disprove. But would you give everything you possess, including that Range Rover of yours parked outside, and all that gold round your neck, round your wrist, round your finger... would you give it all away?"

Moral lowered himself luxuriously into the hot water, so that his gold neck chain, and even his mobile adam's apple, were submerged. "The trouble with you, friend, and you..." turning to me "...sorry, I didn't get your name..." I repeated my name "... is that you are not reading the Scriptures in the true spirit; that is why they don't reveal themselves to you. You take things out of context and then twist them, violate them, to suit your own point of view. It's pathetic really."

"Are you prepared to love your enemy, hate your family, and give everything you own to the poor?"

"See what I mean? May the Lord forgive you."

"If you aren't prepared to do those three things, Jesus has had very little influence in your life."

"By His own blood, I have obtained eternal redemption; let His blood cleanse your consciences from the vile things you have been saying..." all the while those pitying eyes, as blue as a safari suit in the radiance of a summer sky "...and begin to serve the living God. Without the shedding of blood there is no forgiveness. God sacrificed his only begotten son in order to set me... er... us free from the sins we have committed. And let me tell you, masters, my sins, before I committed myself to Jesus and allowed his blood to wash them away, would shock you to the core. Yes, no - to the core of your being."

"What did you do?"

"The lot, master, the lot."

"Drugs?"

"Drugs, sex, violence. Even Communism. I actually admired Garfield Todd before Jesus came into my life! I was going one way, friends, one way."

At that point a German colonial family, five in all, entered the pool and began to dive-bomb each other. Father had a half eaten sausage in his hand, mother blew her nose into the water, and at least one of the children, judging by its sudden stillness, its sudden glazed look, and its sudden shivering, urinated. Bouncer and I decided we had had enough of the healing waters, Moral sidled over to the lower back jet which Amarylis had vacated, and Amarylis began to snore.

"Bloody Huns!" said Bouncer as we made our way to the showers. He would have been too young to fight in the Second World War, but he would have got it all, and more, from his father's generation, the "Battler Briton" comics, and his favourite literary character, Biggles. When we discovered that we were both from Bulawayo (small world) we invited each other to share a six pack of Windhoek lager in our respective apartments situated above the spa complex. We agreed to start in Bouncer's apartment ("While the old girl's asleep and we can have the place to ourselves"), and then to move on to mine.

"Not in the same league as Rhodesian Lion lager," said Bouncer passing me a can of unchilled Windhoek, "but pleasant, nonetheless. Cheers!"

"Good luck!" I replied, and we proceeded to get drunk together.

87

THE AWARD CEREMONY

Two patriots, a glorious son, and a glorious daughter, were to be honoured this sunny late-winter day, July 28, 2007. They were to receive Zimbabwe's second highest civilian merit award: the Tupperware Cross (rust-free, water-resistant, available only at the most respectable retail outlets). And there to pin the medals on his chest and her breast (I'll fumble this one) was none other than the Deputy Minister of Borrowdale Shopping Centre, Comrade Colonel Bolo d'Ingati-Swatibumbum.

The venue was the large city hall in Bulawayo, and it was packed to crumbling capacity. The atmosphere was thick with anticipation and the reek of chicken and chips fried in rancid oil. The recipients sat demurely in the front row watching the entertainment that preceded the award ceremony. Even from my cramped position near the back I could make out that both recipients were in uniform: hers of the nursing profession, and his of the police force. What added to the glamour of the occasion was the indisputable fact that they were a married couple. I had to crane my neck to see that they were actually holding hands.

The proceedings were only two hours late, yet the entertainers were flagged. What could you expect of ten year old girls, clearly malnourished, wearing the skimpiest costumes, and having to keep up with the man who played the *isigubhu* and who doubled (or should I say trebled) as their manager and as tonight's master of ceremonies. He was magnificently arrayed in a leopard skin and a pair of unmistakably Calvin Kline underpants. (I mention these child entertainers because of the tragedy that befalls them in the closing minutes of the ceremony.)

Meanwhile they gyrated their skinny, pre-pubertal bodies in the most suggestive of ways before an audience, which was, by contrast, obese – a sure sign that they were paid-up members of ZANU-PF. One woman was wearing a blouse the size of a double-bed sheet, which sported the slogan: OUR PRESIDENT FOR LIFE. There were slogans on shirts, dresses, and even trousers all over the hall: PASI na BLAIR, PASI na BUSH, PASI na PIOUS; PAMBERI ne ZANU PF, PAMBERI ne CHIMURENGA THREE, PAMBERI ne GRAIN MARKETING BOARD; NO VACANCIES WITHIN THE PRESIDIUM; FORWARD WITH OPERATION DZIKISA MITENGO....

At last, the Minister made his appearance, not, initially, on stage, but accompanying his enormous wife in the separate compartment, known as a box, which is reserved for dignitaries. It is located near the ceiling, stage left, and juts out from the wall like a balcony. The chairs in the box had to be replaced by a large settee in order to accommodate the pretty giantess. She was holding a Kentucky fried drumstick in one hand, and a glass of coca cola in the other. She was wearing a crimson velvet dress, which might once have been stage curtains.

Heads and television cameras swivelled to the right and tilted at an angle of seventy degrees. Feet stamped, hands clapped, tongues ululated, and lips whistled. The guest of honour, resplendent in his bemedalled (sic) army uniform, gave us a smart salute, and proceeded, circuitously, to the stage where he made an hour-long speech condemning those proxies of Blair and Bush who were working with unpatriotic elements to undermine the great and glorious gains of the liberation struggle. He brought down the house with some scurrilous comments about a certain Archbishop (name supplied), and then went into top gear churning out what people even higher than he in the

89

ranks of power, churned out: "The fight against Zimbabwe [he was now reading, somewhat hesitantly, from a script] is the fight against us all. Today it is Zimbabwe, tomorrow it will be South [er] Africa… it will be Mozambique… it will be Angola… it will be any oth [er] African country. And any gov [er] nment that is p [er] ceived to be strong, and to be resistant to imp [er] ialists, will be made a target and will be und [er] mined. So let us not allow any point of weakness in the sol [er] darity of the SADC, because that weakness will also be transf [er] red to the rest of Africa." He used the phrase "sov [er] eign state" no fewer than sixteen times in the course of his diatribe. The audience adored him.

Finally he turned to the purpose of this gathering of party faithful (don't ask me, *mon semblable, mon frere*, what I was doing there) and called the hero and the heroine to the stage. Both kept their heads modestly bowed as they gathered in a comradely fashion on either side of that beautifully pressed uniform with its tinkling medals. Both recipients of the award had shown extreme patriotism in the execution of their duties. By strangling five terminally ill patients at Bulawayo's Ububele Hospital, Comrade Sister Chigaramanhenga had helped to solve the problem of urban overcrowding, in the spirit of the by no means exhausted government initiative, Operation Murambatsvina (clear out the human excrement). By beating so severely, with a metre long rubberized truncheon, and by stomping so energetically with his size twelve hob-nailed boots, seven women supporters of the National Constitutional Assembly, that they later died of their injuries, Comrade Inspector Chigaramanhenga had helped preserve his country's sovereignty in its struggle against Western-backed advocates of regime-change, like whites, coloureds, Indians, and… er… Ndebeles. The fact

90

that the seven women, two of them expectant mothers, had been all Shona, did not seem relevant in the present circumstances.

Then he pinned the medals, first on the police officer, who responded with a smart salute, then (much fumbling here) on the nursing sister, who responded with a delicate curtsey. The audience exploded, and that energy, combined with ministerial bulk (the wife), dislodged the VIP box, and it came crashing down onto the little girls who had danced for us to the point of exhaustion. They had been made to stand under the box in order to watch the award ceremony. All six were killed instantly, but the minister's wife bounced into safety, calling out "Where's my tub of Kentucky fried?"

THE BIG FIVE

It was at Punda Maria where, despite the intrusive Mopani trees and the irritating call of the Cape turtle dove, we got our first sighting. We couldn't believe our good luck. If it wasn't for a herd of impalas leaping idiotically over the road, we might have been able, with our Canon EOS 350D, to play with its shadow, its reflection, its profile. You guessed it: a silver Toyota Land Cruiser Prado VX Turbo Diesel. My hand was shaking when I ticked it on the checklist.

Our two-night stay at the Punda Maria rest camp was all but ruined by the crowds of long-tail cassias, Natal mahoganies, sycamore figs, tamboties, and the ubiquitous mopani. The birds were intolerable, especially that raucous francolin! Even worse, a pack of hyenas insisted on patrolling the boundary fence. But all was not lost, for, parked two tents down from our campsite, was a Range Rover, 3.6 litre, V8 turbo-charged and intercooled diesel engine, glovebox illumination... smell those leather seats... and emblazoned on its rump, the proud words: "Don't try to follow me – you won't make it". We must have photographed it a hundred times.

After Punda Maria we headed south, in our 1978 Datsun with its faded yellow Zimbabwe number plate, towards Shingwedzi and, with the aid of our Zeiss FL (with fluoride glass) we almost completed our checklist: Mazda, Isuzu, Volkswagen, Ford, BMW, Honda, Opel, Nissan, Hundai... you name it. But we were obsessed with the Big Five, and we'd already been fortunate enough to encounter two of them. The famed Kanniedood Drive was a big disappointment because the bush was teeming with game: obnoxious giraffe, silly wildebeest, vain zebra, supercilious kudu.... Even the skies were polluted, with kingfishers, bee eaters, storks, herons and, worst of all, eagles and vultures. At the sight of a ground hornbill waddling along the road with no fewer than three frogs in its repulsive beak, we almost decided to turn around and head for home.

If anything, our camping experience at Shingwedzi was even worse than those disturbed nights in Punda Maria. We had to erect our tent right under an apple leaf tree! The resident birds, none more obnoxious than the glossy starlings and the woodland kingfishers, completely spoiled our sundowner time; and our sleep was disturbed by the yelping of jackals and the eructations of rutting impala. We even had to listen to a leopard coughing. But then peace at last, nay joy, when we heard the arrival of the 'best 4X4 by far', the Landrover Defender 2.5 TDi with Aircon, CD-Radio, Power Steering, Centre Diff Lock/Rear Diff Lock, Customised Safari Equipment. Using our flash, we got in some good shots: from the back, from the front, and from both sides. We managed to get a wonderful close-up of the left back passenger door handle, a picture we intend to frame.

On our way to Balule we were surprised to find that the low-level causeway over the Olifants was under water. We, along with a number of other visitors, were afraid to attempt a crossing in case the powerful current swept us into the disgusting brown river. It seemed as if we had been marooned there for ages, pulling faces at the wire-tailed swallows and the yellow-billed storks, bored stupid by a fight between two male hippos, sickened by the cry of the fish eagle... when a seeming miracle took place. We heard the powerful diesel engine before we witnessed it: a snow white Toyota Fortuner 3.0TD 4X4 with all the mod cons including mp3, Elec. Windows, and Airbags. Almost simultaneously a huge rogue elephant with tusks that ploughed the earth before it, began crossing the causeway from the other side. There is no stopping one of the Big Five, however – except briefly, to engage low gear – and the Fortuner eased onto the causeway. The current swirled about its massive, beautifully treaded wheels as it approached the elephant, now flapping its ears like carpets being dusted. We began to giggle with excited apprehension. Predictably the elephant chickened out and backed away, allowing the Fortuner to cross over to glory. We cheered and cheered, as did the other stranded visitors, all deeply satisfied with our photos of that ineffable vehicle.

After an hour or two the water subsided sufficiently for us to attempt a crossing, and we were mightily relieved to get to the other side. Balule was a most rewarding camp site since we counted no fewer than thirteen white and silver Toyota Hilux Double Cabs within the boundary fence. If there were a sixth Big One, this vehicle would be It. Our disappointments were restricted to a few squirrels and an ugly pair of plum-coloured starlings. Oh, and the far too many Terminalia prunioides with their creamy flowers in slender axillary spikes, their purplish red fruits, and their long, drooping branches.

The next day turned out to be our last because we got to see the last of the Big Five; consequently there was no longer any point in enduring unpleasant scenery: bush, bush, and more bush – especially when it teemed with game. We suspected something dramatic when, on our way to Satara, we saw a herd of buffalo surrounding a male lion, which had been mortally wounded in a battle with a sable antelope. That was on the left side of the road. On the right side a rhino and a leopard had teamed up to fight an elephant, and the result was carnage, enthusiastically welcomed by four species of vulture, a family of hyenas, a pack of wild dogs, a marabou stork, and God knows how many dung beetles. And guess what we saw in the midst of it all? Yes: the rarest and positively the most beautiful (and dangerous) of the Big Five: a Mitsubishi Pajero with Bull Bars, electronically controlled sequential multi-port fuel injection, and a place to hold a can of coke.

THE CARUSO OF COLLEEN BAWN

Hearing all this talk of the Three Tenors put me in mind of a barrel-chested fitter and turner who answered to the curious name of Sigford Bong. We children called him Uncle Siggie, but he was known throughout the South-Western districts as "The Caruso of Colleen Bawn".

We children spent much of our school holidays around the swimming pool up at the club: the boys on their tummies so as to conceal erections; the girls self-conscious in their revealing swim-suits, or "cossies" as we called them. When he was on night duty, which was every other week, Uncle Siggie would join us at the pool and regale us with stories of the adult world: how Kudu White had killed an Aberdeen Angus bull (called Wellington) by punching it on the nose; how Mrs Van Dwap would have won the 1947 Matabeleland Ballroom Dancing championship if she had been wearing panties - the judges lost concentration every time her frock billowed - how so and so (name given) had been caught in the compound "doing it" with a "nanny"! Sex across the colour bar was seen by the white community of Colleen Bawn as a crime worse than serial killing. But his favourite topic of conversation was Caruso...

"Robinson Caruso?"

"No, you idiot, Enrico: the greatest tenor in recording history."

We were much more interested in Pat Boone and Jim Reeves but, like all solipsists, Sigford Bong was highly sensitive, so we humoured him, and listened for the umpteenth time to his no doubt apocryphal anecdotes about Caruso. He had a chest expansion of seventeen inches; he could hit a D-flat in full voice; he could hold a note for so long that crystal chandeliers would tinkle, and once, his voice shattered a wine glass.

"Uncle Siggie, tell us how Crusoe died?"

"Caruso, not Crusoe! I've told you already.

"Please tell it again? Rosie hasn't heard it."

The emulous fitter and turner, with forced reluctance, his voice dropping almost to a whisper, would recall that fateful night when Caruso, in the middle of a glorious and unexpected obligato, which set up a tingling sensation in the bones of the thousand strong audience, burst a blood vessel in his throat and sprayed blood all over the conductor, the first violinist, and several other players in the orchestra. That unsurpassed note collapsed into a gurgle just below middle C, thence to a sigh of arterial bubbles, and the greatest tenor the world had ever known was no more. "The amazing thing," Uncle Siggie continued, "was that his actual death took place exactly when his theatrical death was to take place. So, for quite a while, the audience were unaware that they had witnessed his real death; rather, they took it as a brilliantly executed stage death. Isn't that sad?"

Yes, it is sad, particularly when I recall Siggie's own death, one of the first of the Colleen Bawn crowd to be killed by guerillas, in the Chimurenga.

After chatting with us for a while, Sigford would stroll over to the gents' change room, which was situated next to the ladies' change room, underneath the club balcony, site of many a romantic moonlit moment for the tiny white and whitish community of Colleen Bawn. While changing into his swimming trunks, Sigford would take advantage of the superb acoustics in that chlorine and foreskin scented chamber to regale us, a troop of baboons on the number nine fairway, and the world at large, with a rendering of one of his favourite songs:

"Torn Arse Surrender". Uncle Siggie never knew more than one or two words of the ten or so songs and arias in his repertoire, but he filled in the gaps with bits of fanakalo, Afrikaans, and gibberish and pronounced them in an Italianate way, which we and, presumably, the baboons, not to mention the world at large, found reasonably convincing. The song referred to above came out something like this:

> Video Marie's kunt below!
> mina funa sentimento,
> kom too itchy peperoni,
> enza lo roast o baaie sunny.
> Guava guava shitso intu,
> siente sis aikona hamba;
> nu profuma, mandyricedavies,
> ini wena funa lapa?
> vut seh yay ifarto, addio....

No one really cared about the words when we listened to Sigford Bong's magnificent organ woofing and tweeting through the concrete walls of that acoustical wonder, the gents' change room. Years later, more out of curiosity than genuine interest, I purchased at a flea market in Bulawayo, a long-playing record entitled "Caruso in Song". I listened to the first side and wondered what all the fuss was about: he couldn't hold a candle to old Siggie. Then I poured myself a Vicks Medi-nite and coke and turned the record over. I barely listened to the first song, which was entitled "Manella mia" and which Caruso recorded on January 21, 1914. But the second song took me back, instantly, to my childhood in Colleen Bawn, and I felt tears gather in my eyes. I saw again the mopani scrub after the first rains in late October; saw how the bark darkened and the new leaves opened like butterfly wings smelling faintly of turpentine. The incessant din of Christmas beetles came back to me, lazily interspersed by the distant factory hooter calling the men to work or to knock off. And the baking heat! It was one of Uncle Siggie's songs. I was amazed to see that it was called "I' m'arricordo e Napule" because, out of Sigford Bong's mouth it sounded more like "A merry turd o yeh nipple-ee". It took me back to the Colleen Bawn club, our social centre where we fell in and out of love almost as frequently as we jumped in and out of the swimming pool. The penultimate song on side two confirmed at least one of Uncle Siggie's boasts about Caruso: he could hit a D-flat straight from the chest. I poured myself another Vicks Medi-nite and toasted, in absentia, the Caruso of Colleen Bawn.

It was in 1974, I believe, when Sigford Bong joined the Police Reserve in order to help defend his beloved Rhodesia from the Communist menace. He was soon in demand, giving unaccompanied recitals in the many pubs and "watering holes" that were patronised by the Police Reserve and other Territorials. Of necessity his repertoire grew and he condescended to sing Irish and Scottish songs, still making up most of the words, but holding true to the melodies.

Possibly because he had never received any training, Sigford could not sustain the quality and volume of his voice beyond four or five numbers. After that, especially when he was in his cups, he shouted rather than sang - not that his fellow pub crawlers, shouters themselves, noticed any difference.

When Sigford Bong hit a D-sharp for the first and only time in his life he wasn't in the Gents' change room of the Colleen Bawn club, nor was he in the bar of Tod's Hotel, his favourite wartime haunt: he was in the back of a grey Mazda bakkie riding shotgun, dressed in his navy blue

Police Reserve uniform. There must have been at least a hundred cars in that convoy heading for South African coastal resorts (it was school holidays). We were in the very front of the convoy immediately behind the machine-gun mounted bakkie. We children kept distracting Mr Bong by pulling faces at him and making incomprehensible signs with our hands. He responded by taking his eyes off the menacing bush, his hands off the machine-gun, and his mind off his duty.

It happened so quickly. My father, who was driving our Peugeot 404, stuck his head out of the car window and shouted, "Give us a song, Caruso!" Mr Bong obliged. He crawled away from his position behind the machine-gun all the way to the back of the truck, the better to be heard by us. He managed to shout "Video marie's..." before the bullets of an A K 47 turned his body into a dancing puppet. Out of his expanding gape came a very high, very pure note, accompanied by a spray of frothy blood, which went all over our windscreen. My father turned on the wipers as if this act would somehow negate the fact that the Caruso of Colleen Bawn was no more.

THE CASE OF THE RED BALL POINT PEN

Because the murder weapon was a red ball point pen, suspicions initially fell upon one of the teachers. Teachers have so many motives to kill: their poor pay, their lowly status, their pupils, to mention a few. Then, one of the policemen investigating the case, Inspector Golightly Charamba, was visited by an insight. It must have been the association of colours. A red herring dragged across a fox's path, confuses the dogs (the inspector knew his *Students' Companion*). That was it! The murderer was no school teacher but a cunning pupil or groundsman – or even the sick bay matron! After all she looked like a killer, and everyone knew that there was bad blood between her and the victim, the school bursar. And that, let's not deny it, is where the headmaster, with his hooded lids and protruding eyeballs, looking as if he were about to ejaculate, comes into the picture. Everyone at the… Secondary School, except the headmaster's wife, Foofinks, knew that he had been bonking both women – sometimes in his office, sometimes in the sick bay, but mostly between the far posts on the First Team rugby field. To complicate matters, the body had gone missing from Mpilo mortuary!

This was not going to be an easy case to solve. Make no mistake about that! There were several other suspects with equally compelling motives. There was the Commerce teacher, a poet and aesthete, with tubercular cheeks and a concave back, who was deeply distressed by crimplene, a synthetic, crease-resistant fabric. The bursar swore by crimplene and wore it every day of the week, every Saturday (watching cricket or rugby), and every Sunday (worshipping at The Blood of Jesus Temple).

Then there was the government spy who taught French. He could not bear to have his pay cheques countersigned by an indigenous white woman who once called him a cheeky so and so! And who referred to blacks as "these people". Moreover, he'd been given the farm in Marula which had been owned by the bursar's family for three generations. And the bitch knew it!

And what about the euphemistically called Estate Manager, a blood relation of the bursar's, though a coloured. They claimed the same grandfather, Van Pomp. The bursar had known it though she had denied it.

My motive is that I had no motive (I know my Camus). But I was a suspect because I was the only teacher whose red ball point pen had gone missing. Was that my pen protruding from the bursar's left nostril?

I was mulling over these points on my way home from refereeing a rugby match at the school. My team, the Under 14 Bs had beaten their rivals from Plumtree, and I was feeling well contented. Just opposite the gates to Nesbitt Castle, in Percy avenue, who should come alongside me but Afrika, the staffroom cleaner? Now Afrika and I were pretty good friends, even though he had stolen my lamb's wool scarf, made in Italy, and given it to his wife who wore it as a doek. Forgiving is easier than forgetting.

We exchanged pleasantries, commented on the weather, the political situation, and the price of food, if you could get it. Afrika was on his way to Donnington where a connection had promised to sell him a cow's head at a reasonable price. It would feed his family for a couple of days. He gestured to the woven plastic mealie meal bag on the carrier of his bicycle. It was tied down with strips of rubber tubing.

101

He accompanied me all the way to my turn-off, where we waved goodbye to each other. Afrika still had a long way to go.

Later that afternoon I decided to go on a search for bread. Jaggers was the nearest shop, so I would begin there. I was cycling along Leander Avenue when, on that dangerous S-bend, just before you get to Derby Road, I saw signs of an accident. My heart thumped when I noticed that a bicycle had been involved. You take your life into your hands when you cycle in Bulawayo. Or put it this way: you don't NOT take your life into your own hands.

The car was a pale green Morris Minor 1000. It had been pushed off the road. The police and the ambulance had come and gone but there was a small crowd of shocked local residents standing around. One of them had been a witness and he told me that the driver of the car was a very old white lady who had lost control on the second bend of the S and had crashed into the cyclist. They had both been taken off in the ambulance, and both, apparently, had died: one of injuries sustained, the other of shock.

The bike was mangled, and next to it, still intact, was a woven plastic mealie meal bag with something inside it. The neck of the bag had been tied with a strip of rubber tubing. I told the crowd that the owner of the bike had been a colleague of mine and asked them if they would arrange to carry the bike to Afrika's compound, which was not far away, on the school grounds. I would deliver the bag because I knew what was in it, and I also knew that Afrika had a hungry family to feed. One strapping youth picked up the bike and gestured to me to lead the way.

I was surprised at the relative lightness of the bag when I lifted it and swung it over my shoulder. It felt more like a calf's head than a cow's head. Poor Afrika had been let down by his connection.

We got to the school compound and I asked for Afrika's wife. She came to me, snotty children in her wake, wearing my lamb's wool scarf, made in Italy, on her head. She hadn't yet heard about the accident. I didn't have the courage to tell her; I would leave that to the youth carrying the bicycle, who was some way behind me. I handed the bag over to her and she thanked me. I hurried on my way but not quickly enough to miss the terrible wailing when the youth had broken the news to her.

It must have been about a week later. I was sitting on my own in the staffroom, marking a bunch of essays on the role of Caliban in Shakespeare's *The Tempest*, when I heard a tentative knock on the glass-paned door. I looked up to see one of Afrika's children.

"Yes, umfaan?" I said.

He waved something at me, and then I heard him say "Your pen, mister."

I opened the door and took the pen from the child. It was a red ball point. It could have been mine. It could have been anybody's. We all used the same *Eversharps* at our school. We thanked each other and he returned to the compound while I returned to my marking, wondering whether to tick or to question (the pen still worked) a pupil's point that the name Caliban was an anagram.

THE FANNIED MAN

Until then, Private Spoon's experience of the female member, or "Gentlemen's Passage", as he once heard his mother put it, had been vicarious. He frequently visited the Matopos National Park where he saw, in the configurations of hill and dale, a myriad female parts: bums, bellies, tits and pudenda. And the nutrient smells that wafted from the nooks and crannies of that ancient granitic place; the boulders, themselves once juices of a cooling mass, stuccoed with yellow, orange, grey, green lichen; scent of dassie, baboon, leopard; sponges halfway up Efifi, still, months after the rains, discharging dark water to trickle down veins and along dykes in search of cracks, which sprout mosses, ferns, resurrection plant… all this, and much more, filled him with an aching desire to experience the female member.

He frequently went into town, at busy times, so that he could watch girls and young women as they crossed the streets and walked along the pavement. His favourite place in Bulawayo was the corner of Eighth Avenue and Fife Street – outside the public lavatories where he could melt into the busy traffic of vendors, tourists, micturaters, and local shoppers. He had eyes only for the oval office, mons veneris, straining to make out that shape, like the head of a barbel, but each one minutely different. Windy days brought him occasional treats, glimpses of panties when skirts flapped, which would make him gasp with desire; and jeans, so tight against the flesh as to throw into relief, though not bring relief, that other landscape, that clamminess, that "boggy acre" enfolded, cloven, reaching back to the limbus, back to the games of Gargantua: at the O wonderful, the soilie smutchy, fast and loose, bush leap, break pot, battabum….

Then he discovered fannies all over his own body, which he would ogle for minutes at a time; some he even touched, fingered, abused with pencils and ballpoint pens. He would bend his arms at the elbow and instantly, four fannies appeared, two hairy on top, and two bald beneath; he would bend his leg at the knee and four larger more engorged fannies would appear; with a little muscle control he could make them flex, yield, contend. Between his fingers and toes he discovered tiny, nonetheless interesting fannies that would not look amiss between the legs of a Barbie doll, or even a human midget. He noticed and then studied diverse fannies on his face: his dimpled chin, the frown on his forehead, the corners of his eyes, his lips, the parting between his earlobes and his neck. He became reckless and thought of his anus as a fanny. He inserted all manner of penis-like objects until pain overwhelmed desire. Finally he transformed his own genitalia into a fanny by tucking them between his legs and squeezing his thighs together until only a delta of crinkly hair remained visible. Until then.

It would soon be his turn; a chance to see a real vulva. He felt his heart pounding against his ribs, and his breath came short. He shifted his weapon to the other shoulder. The girl was humped against an upturned wheelbarrow, and at every lunge the wheel would creak, and she would flop like a doll. She had stopped making a sound and he wondered if she was still conscious, still alive! He fixed his eyes on some vultures circling above them. He thought they might be Cape vultures since they were very pale. He remembered, as a child, watching vultures at a carcass on the banks of the Shashi River. How they danced around with comical hops, wings outspread, too engorged with offal to take off.

The soldier in front of him shuddered and then rolled away from the girl. Somebody prodded him from behind. "I just want a look," he

105

said to no one in particular, "that's all — just a look, tra la la." Two of us grabbed him by the combat jacket, called him a wanker, and flung him out of the way. When he tried to stand, my boot caught him on the side of his head, and he cried out. I returned to my place in the queue, somewhat out of breath for the exertion.

THE KEYS

r and Mrs Box, an elderly couple who depended on the Western Union to see them through their twilight – "when the lights are low" – year(s), were taking a walk, she hobbling, he tottering, round the block when they came upon a commotion at Number 43, one of the few properties in the neighbourhood, which had not succumbed to durawalls. Two women were having a game of tug o' war with a rolled up Persian carpet; another two were wrestling, in the Ancient Greek style (though not naked), over a television set; yet another two were screaming at each other for pulling a plastic shower curtain in half. From a pair of very good quality San Sui speakers blared a type of township music known as *Mbaqanga*. An elderly man dressed in typical colonial cookboy's uniform: soft head-covering, khaki shirt and shorts, white apron, bare feet, seemed to be holding court. He sat at a formica table of the type commonly used in Zimbabwean kitchens for the rituals of egg, bacon, sausage, fried tomato, toast, marmalade, and tea – known the world over as an English breakfast. At his elbow stood a bottle of altar wine and a bottle of Dimple Haig Scotch whisky. The Box couple at the gate watched in amazement as the Master of Ceremonies at this yard sale-cum-*pungwe* poured a healthy tot of Dimple Haig into an empty jam tin, filled it with altar wine, and then proceeded to sip it like tea. The illusion of tea was enhanced when he reached over for a matzo wafer, dunked and chewed, sipped, dunked and chewed, sipped... and he went on dunking and chewing and sipping until – Mrs Box counted seven, Mr Box counted eight; they argued about it later – all the wafers were finished. People were coming and going, not through the gate where the Boxes stooped, but through a hole in the fence. A merry fire was blazing on the lawn, fuelled with what looked like Oregon pine ceiling boards, and around which was gathered a number of men roasting roasts – topside, silverside, fillet, leg of lamb, saddle of lamb – Mrs Box also thought she saw a sirloin, while Mr Box noticed that there was none of his favourite: crackling pork.

The Boxes had been doing this walk ever since Vincent's retirement. He had been senior partner at a well known firm of attorney's Cohen, Cohen, and St Cohen. They had lived very comfortably off his generous pension, until the Zimbabwean currency had collapsed. Luckily for them – "and the flick'ring shadows" - their children, Boxy who lived in Australia, and Biggy who lived in Canada, sent them money every month via the Western Union, which had long surpassed Anglo American and Bulawayo's Vapostori as Zimbabwe's major foreign currency earner. Their walk took in a block of sixteen properties, all of which, when the Boxes began the routine, had been occupied by white families. Twelve years later, four of the properties had been turned into Guest Houses, aka brothels, by absentee emergent businessmen with strong ZANU-PF connections; five of them were now occupied by anything up to ten black families (the poorest living in wooden garden sheds and converted swimming pools); two of them had become used, very used, and unbelievably used car "showrooms" catering to the informal sector; four of them belonged to the nephew of a highly connected aunt, which his friends house sat for him until his triumphant return (to be announced) from London; and one of them, Number 43, still belonged to the Newman family who had owned it and lived in it since 1895.

The only remaining member of the Newman family, old Ruth: mother of four, grandmother of seven, and great grandmother of twelve, all, all in other countries across the globe: was confined to a wheelchair. As they continued on their walk, the Boxes worried about Mrs Newman, alone in that house, old and infirm. They decided to telephone her once they got home, and ask if they could help in any way. Her number was in the directory, the only Newman left in Bulawayo. Mr Box dialled; he was answered almost immediately: "Jerry, is that you?"

"Er, no, it's …"

"Stanley? Why don't you call anymore?"

"No, Mrs Newman, I'm a neighbour… name of Box. I just thought…"

"What? You just thought what?"

"Er… will you phone if you need help? Number's 024672… I…we —

"Please get off the line? Off! Get off! I vunt for to shpeak mit my son, the doctor!" Ruth's Yiddish accent was never far below the surface. Her husband, Paul Newman, had met and married her in Vienna, in 1934, and brought her back to the family home in Bulawayo, where they had flourished until the late nineteen sixties when they began to feel threatened by the *schwartze* and, one by one, left. Only Ruth and her husband, Paul, stayed on, Ruth in Number 43 and Paul in the Jewish cemetery at Athlone. The remainder and the remains.

The phone came crashing down in Vincent's left ear, and he gave his wife a shoulder shrug. Then, almost immediately, the phone rang: "Yes, hello, 042672?

"Er… speaking."

"Mister… I am afraid… please… I am very afraid. Please come help. He - " the phone came crashing down.

She's in trouble," said Vincent to his wife Melody, "let's go."

109

They didn't "go", not even "softly"; they tottered and hobbled to the gate of number 43 where their requests to be let in were ignored by the Master of Ceremonies. He was still at the formica table sipping from his jam tin and digging bits of matzo from his teeth with a match stick. He reeked of a combination of 4 7 11 *eau de Cologne* and Yardleys English Lavender, which mingled with the smell of roasting meat, and on the first digit of the little finger of his left hand – stuck there – was a diamond almost as big as the Ritz.

So they went, along with everyone else, through the hole in the fence. "We've come to visit the madam" said Melody to no one in particular, and no one in particular listened to her. But he watched them: all the way up the red cement steps, on to the red cement verandah, through the open front door, along the Rhodesian teak floor boards of the passage way: he watched them.

"Mrs Newman!" called Melody anxiously.

And then Vincent – "though the heart be weary" – "Mrs Newman?"

They wandered about this musty shell of a house, it was almost empty of furnishings, calling for the old lady. "Here. I'm here," they finally heard, and they traced her voice to a closed in porch.

"Knock knock! Mrs Newman?"

"Come in, please?"

She was in her wheelchair, surrounded by medicines in bottles, jars and boxes. She had the frightened eyes of a hunted animal, and she stank of incontinence and neglect. Both Boxes had to work hard to suppress their vomit reflexes.

She had a large bunch of keys hanging from her neck. The bunch was adorned with a faded blue silk ribbon. She was about to speak when a presence, laid up in lavender, materialised at the porch

110

entrance. The look of appeal on Ruth Newman's face changed to a look of terror. One hand clutched the keys on her bosom, while the other raised itself in a feeble attitude of defence. Then, from the back of her throat, came these words, each one half strangled: "I vunt you should pleez go. *Weg, weg...bitte weggehen.*"

The old couple went, watched all the way to the hole in the fence, and laboured –"sad the day and long" – back to their own home where they comforted themselves with a pot of tea and a plate of ginger snaps.

A week or so later, the Boxes were stocking up with groceries at the local supermarket when they came across Mrs Newman's "cook boy". He was pushing a trolley laden with imported luxuries, prominent among them being bottles of Scotch whisky. Melody counted five; Vincent counted six (later they would argue about it); but what most drew their attention was the bunch of keys, adorned with a faded blue ribbon, which dangled from his wiry old neck.

THE LUNCH HOUR

Michelle heard that expression of Rhodesian authority, the car hooter, going long before the hazardous crossing at Cecil John Rhodes Avenue. Come to think of it, all crossings in Bulawayo are hazardous: you might encounter a commuter minibus driven by a teenager with an armed tout in lieu of a driver's licence; an army lorry driven by a soldier with no immune system; a Santana (Spanish equivalent of the Land Rover) driven by a policeman bulging out of his uniform, loaded with hind quarters, fatalistic chickens, and Castle lagers - with assorted ladies taking up the slack; a leaking water bowser on wheels going slower than a tractor; worse, an Octogenarian with blue rinsed hair and a flame-lily brooch, her spectacles, thanks to osteoporosis, just clear of the dashboard of her 1950 Morris Minor; worst of all, you might encounter a Mercedes Benz, and Mercedes Benz drivers – don't they know it – are above the law of the road.

Invoking her St Christopher (she wore it on a silver chain around her neck), and readying her hands to pull the brakes on both wheels of her Raleigh Bomber, Michelle crossed Cecil John Rhodes Avenue without so much as a bent spoke, and sighed with relief. It was lunch hour in suburbia. Little clusters of domestic workers could be seen on the verges next to the driveways of the houses where they worked. She knew each of them and gave each cluster a self-conscious wave as she pedalled by. They waved back with friendly stares.

Yes, it was Mrs Bangle, hooting away for the "boy" to open the gate, her Mazda 626 station wagon loaded with groceries from Haddon & Sly, her dog, Nuisance, sitting on the passenger seat and staring straight ahead Michelle had seen Mishek, barefoot in his blue overalls enjoying his lunch break with fellow domestic workers, in the partial shade of a late flowering Jacaranda, outside number 23 where the Van Deventers lived, which was more or less over the road from where Mrs Bangle lived. Mishek could hear the "madam" parp-parping away but he was no longer going to interrupt his lunch break to open the gate for her. This was the nineties not the fifties.

When she drew alongside the station wagon, Michelle slowed down and looked at Mrs Bangle and her dog through the rear windscreen. They had similar occupants; for a brief moment Michelle wondered why the dog was behind the wheel; then she noticed the ears. She decided to help Mrs Bangle so she got off her bike, leant it against the nearest tree, and approached Mrs Bangle's side window.

"Hi Mrs Bangle," she said, "can I open the gate for you?"

"You can but you may not!" she followed every second syllable with a hoot.

"It's not a problem, Mrs Bangle," said Michelle with one hand on the gate latch.

"Young lady I'm warning you ... do not open the gate." Nuisance growled. "After all I've done for that ingrat... how dare he!"

Michelle decided to appeal to Mishek. She left her bike where it was and walked over to the Van Deventers' driveway. She kept her head down until she was near enough to speak to Mishek.

"Yes, Michelle, *uthini?*"

"*Ngiyaphila.* Er, Mishek, aren't you going to open the gate for Mrs Bangle? She's -"

"What is the time Michelle?"

"She looked at her wrist watch: "It's ten to two."

"My lunch break ends at two; at two I will open the gate for Mad."

"But Mishek..."

Languidly chewing on a stem of blonde grass, moved from a sitting position to a reclining position, using his elbows as struts so he could face Michelle, he said, "Go tell the madam that I will open the gate at two." His tone was sardonic. Then he spoke to his companions in iSindebele, too quickly for Michelle to follow, and they all burst out laughing.

Michelle, faced flushed, walked back to the Mazda 626. A carbon monoxide effluvium made her wrinkle her nose. She was quite breathless when she addressed Mrs Bangle's hairdo: a severe imperishable perm, determinedly off the neck, which reeked of hair spray.

"He says he will open the gate when his lunch break ends at two."

"Who the devil does he think he is!" parp parp! "Of all the -" parp! " It's so -" parp par-parp!

"Please Mrs Bangle, it's so -"

"Whose side are you on anyway?"

"Yours ...I mean no one's ... it's just -"

Parp pa parp parp! Dogs from all over suburbia joined in the commotion. Then illegal roosters began to make their contribution. Somewhere a kettle whistled.

"Just what? miss clever Dick."

"I'm sorry... I'll..."

"Go and tell that so-and-so that there will be no Christmas box for him this year... no more hand-me-downs... no more turning a blind eye to all the sugar he steals, not to mention the coffee and the alcohol and the deodorant." Parp parp parp!

Michelle shrugged her shoulders and walked slowly back to Misheck who was now lying on his stomach, gently drumming his backside with his heels. "Misheck, she says you won't get a Christmas box this year…"

"So I have to do without the small tin of mixed fruit jam, the tobacco, which I don't smoke, the cheap sweets, the cheap biscuits the cheap tea, and the bar of green Sunlight soap. How terrible." He said this to his companions and they all laughed. "I used to get a small bottle of Mazoe orange as well but that has become too expensive for the madam who drinks Liquifriut imported from South Africa."

Parp parp parp!

She was talking to the back of his head. "She said some other things too…"

"Tshela mina."

Parp pa parp parp!

"Taking things without asking…"

Pa parp parp!

"Such as?"

Michelle hesitated too long before saying: "You know… sugar and stuff like that."

Parp!

"I cannot afford to buy sugar on the wage she pays me." He turned over and raised his head to face her. They were about the same age, seventeen or so. *"Hamba Michelle, hamba ekhaya."*

"Phepha, Mishek."

"Kuhle, Michelle."

Once again Michelle retraced her steps to Mrs Bangle. A number of residents in the vicinity came to their gates to restrain their dogs and see what all the fuss was about, saw Mrs Bangle pounding her hooter, shook their heads, clicked their tongues, and returned to whatever it was that they did during the lunch hour. Michelle was alarmed to see

115

that Mrs Bangle was weeping. Her mascara stained cheeks made her look, if one didn't look too hard and long, like a circus clown. Her countenance was beginning to collapse, her hairdo, however held firm. Nuisance whined and licked her nearest ear.

"Mrs Bangle," she said gently. Mrs Bangle burst into tears. The sunspots all over her visible flesh began to dance, and Michelle realized that she, too, had begun to weep. "Mrs Bangle..." but all she received was a spondee of parps.

Michelle looked at her watch: only two or three minutes to the end of the lunch hour. "Hold on, Mrs Bangle," she sobbed, "he'll be here soon." She noticed that some of the domestic workers along the road were getting up and dusting themselves; not Mishek, however.

Then Mrs Bangle spoke. Michelle could barely make out the words, three words, repeated like the hooting of a car: "It's all over. It's all over." Then two words: "All over. All over." Then one word "Over". Finally, the ejaculation: "O... o... o...". Without invitation, a Roy Orbison song found its way into Michelle's consciousness. Guiltily she stuttered a good-bye to Mrs Bangle, climbed on her bike and pedalled away. When she got to her gate on the next block the hooting had become continuous.

That's how Mishek found her, on his way, now that the lunch hour was over, to open the gate. Her head had slumped onto the hooter in the middle of the steering wheel. Nuisance had buried his nose in her lap. He was whimpering. Gently Mishek lifted the head off the hooter and cut the over-heated engine. As soon as he lifted the head it flopped back onto the steering wheel. Mishek was not convinced that she was dead. Once more, gripping the stiff perm, he lifted the head. What he saw filled him briefly with panic: her lifeless grey eyes stared at him, through him; and her normally tight mouth hung spittily slack and open. For a second she returned to life when a dolorous sigh escaped her body. He let go the head and went to open the gate for her. His next task was to weed the little patch of lawn that she had made him keep alive with bath and sink water; then he would feed Nuisance and the two cats, top up the water in the bird bath, polish madam's shoes, turn the compost... and that should bring him to knock off time when he would be free to seek out Michelle and give her the sad news.

THE PASSPORT OFFICE

I did not realise, until I had to apply for a new passport, what an arduous, self-destroying job it is to work in a passport office. These people are saints and ought to have their salaries quadrupled and their working hours cut by half.

I took off an entire morning from work in order to queue for an application form. Imagine my surprise, not to mention gratitude, when, in less than five hours, I had received my form. True, I paid a professional "queuer" $80 000 to help me skip 487 places, and true, I was engrossed in a James Hadley Chase novel, but still! My compliments to the Bulawayo passport office for moving the queue along so briskly.

When I returned the next day, with my completed form and my $50 000, I was quite rightly turned away from the door by a clearly overworked (judging by the way he was yawning) official. You see, it was almost 3 p.m.; the passport office was justified in closing its doors to a tardy member of the public.

At this point I applied for a week's leave from work so that I could devote all my time and attention to the acquisition of a new passport. On the third day I arrived good and early and was allowed to join another queue. There was one official in attendance and her work was so arduous, processing carelessly filled-in application forms, that she had to take a five-minute break after every form. Those of us standing in one of the queues in what must be one of the dirtiest, most run-down buildings in the Southern hemisphere, clicked our tongues in sympathy. She would wander around the building chatting to those colleagues of hers who were also on five-minute breaks, speaking to her boyfriend on the telephone, and taking swigs from a bottle of, no doubt tepid, coca cola.

It seemed like no more than the wink of an eye when, three hours later, I was face to face with the good lady. She checked my papers, looked at my passport photo and burst out laughing. She took my photograph to all the other officials not in attendance, held it before their tired eyes, pointed at me and shrieked with laughter. Those of us in the various queues were deeply moved by the way these martyrs to bureaucracy consoled each other and we did not begrudge them a laugh at our expense. They needed all the morale-boosting they could get.

It turned out that the photograph was clean-shaven while I had a beard of three days' growth. The official would not accept this and told me to come back with another photograph. I suggested shaving but she stuck to her guns, the noble creature.

Two days later, on my fourth visit to the passport office, I stood in the queue for over an hour before anybody came to attend to us. The same official emerged from somewhere in the bowels of the building, a Chelsea bun in one hand, a bottle of coke in the other, and took up her post at the desk. She snapped her fingers for the first set of papers and then, unaccountably, got up and walked slowly away. Just like that! Poor thing: she must have been on the verge of a nervous break down. What do you expect, toiling under these harsh conditions?

Someone else, a gentleman, eventually took over our queue, eventually checked my papers, and I nearly died of gratitude when he accepted them and sent me to the cashier. Another queue, but not so long. Unfortunately for the "queuers", however, but most understandably for the beleaguered cashier, there was a very pretty girl with him who insisted on being chatted up; so it was at least another hour before I handed in my forms and paid my $50 000. "Come back in a year's time," the cashier said to me, and I almost giggled with gratitude.

THE STONE PAINTER

His name is Farlow, and he paints the stones, dressed and raw, and the bricks, full and half, in the grounds of the police headquarters at the Drill Hall. His uniform is a khaki shirt, khaki shorts, car tyre sandals, and a red, tasselled fez. Farlow is a Muslim of Malawian extract. He began work at the Drill Hall some time in the 1950s. He was, by turns, tea boy, errand boy, and garden boy. It was part of the last mentioned job to whitewash the bricks and the stones, some random, some encircling trees, some delineating roads and pathways and herbaceous borders, some marking out jealously guarded parking space for the more senior police officers.

His first employers were the British South Africa Police who kept law and order for a Chartered Company called Rhodesia. His present employers are the Zimbabwe Republic Police who keep law and order for a Limited Company called ZANU-PF. His first employers gave him a black 28 inch bicycle. For greater comfort, he inserted a tennis ball under the saddle. The bicycle was commandeered by his present employers during Operation Murambatsvina when they were desperately short of transport to pursue prostitutes and street vendors. Now he walks everywhere.

During the Chartered Company years he kept his eyes lowered in the course of duty and pretended not to notice the way constables barely out of their teens would insult suspected law breakers old enough to be their mothers and fathers.. He pretended not to hear the cries, the groans, the pleas for mercy. How did that song go? Those boys from the Support Unit used to sing over their mugs of Tanganda tea, disregarding him on the floor among their boots, polishing, brush in one hand, cloth in the other, Cobra wax, in ever diminishing circles. That smell; and that tune fixing itself in his memory like an ear-worm. Those offensive words:

I came to a river
and couldn't get across,
so I climbed on a nigger
'cos I thought he was a hoss -
kooma-rai-ai-ai-yai-yai,
kooma-rai-kooma-rookie-kooma-kai.

In those days everything at the Drill Hall worked, from the petrol
lawn mower to the electric kettle. There were no smashed light fittings,
no leaking taps, no cracked toilet bowls. The ceilings hadn't fallen
through, the window panes weren't plugged with newspaper, the fixed
benches hadn't been ripped out of the walls. Above all, the Olivetti
typewriters clacked away, with newly inked ribbons, and an endless
supply of foolscap. There were paper clips everywhere, and drawing
pins, and rubber bands, and manila envelopes. There were steel filing
cabinets, brass hooks on the doors for the policemen to hang their
caps, government-issue hand towels. Farlow kept the rooms spotless,
and he had unlimited access to soaps, polishes, and detergents to keep
them that way. And in the yard he dared the weeds to grow, manicured
the lawn, pruned the shrubs, dead-headed the flowers, and painted the
stones.

Now, in the Limited Company years, he no longer keeps his eyes
down, and he no longer pretends not to listen to the cries, the groans,
the pleas for mercy. It passes the time, since there is nothing much to
do. Once the daily *Chronicle* has been read, re-read, and pored over by
the entire unit (who have stopped typing reports on the one remaining
typewriter, which is without ink for its ribbon and without paper for its
battered keys), he uses it to plug holes. In the rainy season he catches
rainwater leaks with the three last remaining utensils: an *Olivine* oil tin, a
two litre plastic *Lions Dairy Maid* ice cream container, and a *Chibuku*
scud. Mostly, however, and whitewash still seems to be available, he
paints the stones; and while he paints, that tune comes back to him,

122

and you can hear the cracked old voice going: "Kooma-rai-ai-ai-yai-yai...kooma-rai-kooma-rookie-kooma-kai,"

THE SUICIDE BOMBER

Ali van Baba could moralise at length on the subject of pork; on the subjects of alcohol and adultery he was a little more circumspect. For you and me pork is no big deal; it's a sausage or a slice of polony or a side of bacon; but for Ali van Baba, Bulawayo's first, and to date, only suicide bomber, pork was a very big deal. Okay, it divideth the hoof and cheweth the cud, like cows and sheep and goats; but did cows delight in filth and dung? Did sheep? Did goats? No, people who eat pork live for the lusts of the flesh. Pigs are insatiable. They ejaculate by the pint. They gobble up everything you put before them. How did that poet, whatshisname, put it:

> They chop a half-moon clean out.
> They eat cinders, dead cats.

What's more, they are carriers of the hairlike nematode worm, which causes trichinosis in humans, and in Ali van Baba's view, any human who eats pork deserves the affliction.

Offensive books like *Mein Kampf* and *The Satanic Verses* and *The Da Vinci Code* couldn't hold a candle, in Ali Van Baba's opinion, to "The Three Little Pigs", not to mention all those stupid nursery rhymes that cutesified the abominations: "And there in a wood a piggy-wig stood...." Sick! Ali van Baba had a mantra, and it went like this: "and he huffed, and he puffed, and he blew their house down"

It was his disgust for pork (and for other things about which he was a little more circumspect), which turned mild-mannered, retiring Ali Van Baba into a suicide bomber. And he it was who invented what has now come to be known as the strapless bomb. The explosive he made from an old IRA recipe and he attached the device to the front of his body by means of three suction pads, one on each nipple, and one, somewhat larger, on the belly button. He shortlisted three possible targets: the mosque on the Harare road (because its onion domes were painted a lurid green), the synagogue in Kumalo (because they wouldn't allow him to pee in their flower bed) and the Blood of Jesus Christian church on the Old Esigodini Road (because it looked like a miniature Jaggers Wholesale building, which is constructed not of straw, nor of sticks, nor of bricks, but of state of the art zinc). Then he applied the pork test. Muslims eschewed the flesh of swine; Jews too, the tempting aroma of grilling bacon notwithstanding; but Christians, most of them anyway, loved it. So pork made him decide, finally, on the last named institution; pork - and practicality.

You see, Ali Van Baba had decided on the wooden horse trick to lure his victims to their destruction. If he chose the mosque, he would leave outside its gate a styrofoam camel on wheels, with him hidden inside. If he chose the synagogue, he would leave outside its gate, a giant bagel, with him inside (the cream cheese, so to speak). He couldn't, at first think of an equivalent lure for the church. A giant jar of home-made jam? No. A giant pot plant? No. A giant braai pack? Maybe. Then it came to him... of course... two birds with one stone... a giant piggy bank. Most Christians ate pork; and judging by the Pajeros and double cabs that patronised this church, they weren't averse to money. A piggy-bank wooden horse would be easier to construct than camel or bagel wooden horses, so he set to work, and before long he had constructed a piggy bank large enough for him and his strapless bomb to hide inside.

Sure enough, it worked. One dark Saturday night, under cover of an overcast sky, whispering, 'he huffed and he puffed, and he blew their house down', Ali van Baba, wearing his strapless bomb and a matching pair of blue overalls, wheeled the porcine contraption all the way from his home in downtown Bulawayo to the gate of the Blood of Jesus Christian church. It took him hours, and along the way he psyched himself up by repeating his mantra, and by muttering: 'Three cheers for the big bad wolf! Down with the piggywig who was willing to sell his ring for a shilling. Down with Porky. Down with Petunia. Down with the old person of Bray who fed figs to his pigs.' He climbed into the piggy bank through an ingeniously constructed trap door under its curly tail. Then he made himself as comfortable as possible and waited, eyes fixed on the coin slot above him, which grew progressively lighter. The first service would begin around 8 a.m. the next day.

He must have fallen asleep because the sound of excited voices took him by surprise. Then he began to move: through the gate, along the ground a way, up a ramp – the voices were growing in numbers and volume – into the warehouse of a building, and then up towards the holier end. He began to fondle the button, which would detonate the bomb. 'He huffed,' he whispered, 'he puffed… and he blew their house down.' There was a commotion about him. Suddenly a loud voice called for order, and order there was, and in those seconds of awed silence, Bulawayo's first and, it is to be hoped, only, suicide bomber, pushed the button. Damn the IRA! Only the detonator went off, blowing Ali Van Baba out of the trapdoor, the pig's vent, where he was received with rapturous applause by the congregation. Then that same voice, which had silenced the flock, announced in tremulous tones that the Second Coming was at hand.

THE VERY HIGH RANKING SOLDIER'S WIFE

The very high ranking soldier's wife shops at The Neglected Lady, which specializes in garments for very large, extremely large, and enormous wives. She likes to dress in what has come to be known as the "late Rhodesian" style. The fabric of choice for this style is crimplene, which, as its name suggests, is corrugated with small folds, like wrinkles. Crimplene is an extremely resistant fabric; it comes in four colours: bubble gum pink, peppermint green, mustard yellow, and heavenly blue.

When it comes to accessories, the very high ranking soldier's wife is fussy about hats and handbags but not about shoes. Her role model, when it comes to hats, is the First Lady, who wears hats that can become converted to ocean-going yachts – should that need ever arise. Her taste in handbags is somewhat eccentric for one of the wealthiest women in Zimbabwe, but it is true to the "late Rhodesian" style, which swears by plastic and press studs, the shinier and clickier the better. As for footwear, her tonnage gives the very high ranking soldier's wife no choice but to go for comfort rather than style. No one except, presumably, her husband, her husband's friend the Minister, her security guard, and her garden boy, has ever seen her without her trusty air-cushioned Reeboks.

When the very high ranking soldier's wife received her money from the now defunct War Veterans Compensation fund – for injuries sustained during the Second Chimurenga (loss of appetite I believe it was) – she spent it wisely. She bought a bottle store from a Greek patriot (as long as he didn't have to live in Greece) in one of Harare's suburban shopping centres. She employed one of her impoverished relatives to run the store, and she sat back and raked in the profits – nothing on the scale of her husband's diamond dealings in the D.R.C. – but pretty substantial, if you ask me. Between them the very high ranking soldier and his wife could live quite comfortably in the "late Rhodesian" style.

They bought a palatial home in Harare's exclusive Mt Pleasant suburb. The previous occupants, a patriotic Scottish couple (as long as they didn't have to live in Scotland), had gone ethnic in a big way, and the first task of the very high ranking soldier's wife was to get rid of the tasteless basket work, animal carvings, soapstone statues, weld art, gourds, skins, and beads that cluttered the place, stank of poverty, and gathered dust. In came the copper fire screen painted with flame lilies; the pot plants ranging from African violets to aspidistras; the porcelain ducks; the chiming clock; Tretchikof's "Weeping Rose"; and tartan anti-macassars for the mustardy-gold lounge suite.

The garden was even more of a challenge for the very high ranking soldier's wife. What kind of a property owner are you that you allow your lawn to grow right up to the jacarandas? Her garden boy's second task was to dig beds around the trees and plant them with marigolds and mother-in-law's tongue. The beds must then be lined with half-bricks, which have been thoroughly whitewashed. Have you no concept of the "late Rhodesian" style, for goodness' sake? She reluctantly kept the hi-biscus hedge since it was, after all, slightly more "late Rhodesian" than instarect walls.

Where she differed with anything Rhodesian, early or late, was in her choice of domestic pets. No overweight, spayed Labradors for the very high ranking soldier's wife; no overweight, castrated ginger toms. She acquired five vicious guard dogs from a bankrupt security firm, chained them up all day, and let them loose all night. Within weeks they

128

had killed and half eaten her garden boy's little sister. Serves her right for trespassing!

The happiest day of her life came when the very high ranking soldier's wife was given one of the most productive commercial farms in Zimbabwe. The racist white occupiers had the effrontery to protest. I mean! Fucksake! *Chave! Chave Chimurenga!* When will these people realise that the land is ours, and that they stole it from us? The racist white couple were in their late seventies so it wasn't too difficult to chase them away, what with the help of the police, the local governor, the war vets, and the "green bombers". The two old land grabbers were given such a hiding that they had to be hospitalized for a fortnight. Mrs Wordsworth still hasn't recovered the use of her sphincter, and Mr Wordsworth is permanently deaf in one ear. As for their pets: they were soaked in paraffin and set alight. Talk about fireworks!

The three hundred or so farm workers and their families, most of whom had been born on the farm, took to their heels after their huts were burnt down, and squatted on the verges of public roads, and in the caves of leopard-infested koppies, until they were set-upon by ZANU-PF youths and driven even further afield. As far as I know, those who haven't died of exposure are still on the run.

What really incensed the very high ranking soldier's wife was that a number of items from the farmhouse was stolen by the racist whites. Apparently they sneaked back to the farm in the company of their son, who had come all the way from New Zealand to console them, and stole, among other things, a silver tea set, which had belonged to Mrs Wordsworth's great grandmother, a set of World War 2 service medals, and three photograph albums, one of them leather bound!

She hired two teenage war veterans, a fifty-year old ZANU-PF youth, and half a dozen pre-adolescent Border Gezi graduates wearing academic gowns over their green boiler suits. They all piled into one of her Pajeros and made a bee-line for the "safe house" where the not-so-safe Wordsworths were waiting in the vacant servant's quarters for death or senility to relieve them of their misery.

The very high ranking soldier's wife and her entourage stormed into the one-room shack, dragged the old folk from their makeshift bed, and forced them to toyi toyi in the yard, shouting ZANU-PF slogans, singing liberation songs from the 70s, until they collapsed in a heap on top of each other. One of the teenage war veterans ordered them to make sex, but the magnanimous very high ranking soldier's wife said that was not necessary. Instead she ordered them to get up and to stand to attention in front of her. She verbally abused them for a few minutes, calling them thieves, homosexuals and racists. Then she demanded that they return her property: the silver tea set, the World War 2 service medals, and the photograph albums.

The erstwhile land grabbers handed over the loot. The very high ranking soldier's wife was particularly taken with the silver tea set, and she promised the Wordsworths that as soon as she had settled at the farmhouse she would invite them to tea.

THE WEIGHT LOSER

Dutch Willy was desperate to lose weight. He was thinking of beginning an affair, after years of celibacy, which had reduced his testosterone level to the point that the only visible muscle on his entire body was that which twitched below his left eyelid. The worst of it was his paunch: it flowed over his belt like excited bread dough. His namesake had disappeared from view, and he could get no more than a peep out of his kneecaps.

He had tried dieting but he was too fond of beer and fatty beef biltong to persevere. He had tried serial vomiting but he could not bear the taste of bile, nor the indignity of kneeling before a lavatory bowl. He had even tried exercise, but the boredom of its routine stupefied him. AIDS was out of the question.

Then an idea came to him. He recalled how thin his gardener, McKenzie, had got after he had spent a week in the police holding cell at..... Station in Bulawayo, Zimbabwe's second city. Prisoners were remanded there until they went before a magistrate to be tried. According to the law, prisoners were not allowed to be kept in a holding cell for longer than twenty four hours but this was ignored by the local police. Some of the prisoners had been there for months. One man, who hailed from the rural areas, had been in that holding cell for three years before dying. He had stolen a tin of baked beans.

Dutch Willy knew just what to do to get into that holding cell. He would insult the President in a public place; public places swarmed with informers. He chose the bar of the Selborne Hotel in Leopold Takawira Avenue. He hadn't been in that bar since the good old

131

Rhodesian days when the only black people allowed in were barmen and barmen's assistants. It was called "The King's Head".

Now he was the only white person in that crowded bar, sitting near the till where the solid teak counter swerved to the left, straightened out for a couple of metres, then swerved again to the left, finally terminating at Pensioners' Corner, tonight the domain of five vociferous young men with newspapers under their arms, and a jabbing tendency in their forefingers. On the wall behind the glans-shaped heads of the young men, he strained his eyes to make out the details of a large framed cheque from some fictitious bank, made out to Pensioners' Corner, and signed Al K. Holic. The amount was for $15 000. A tidy sum in 1988, the year the cheque had been signed. 24 - 6 - 88. Shit, wasn't that his youngest child's date of birth? Talk about coincidences!

He drained his third beer and wondered whether the time was ripe to insult the President. He'd have to shout to be heard above the din. He looked about him, not too brazenly, and counted seven men wearing dark glasses, a sure sign that they were plain-clothed policemen or members of the notorious C.I.O. Give it a bit more time.

He caught sight of his face in the mirror behind the barman, and he suddenly felt tired, ready for bed, or a long hot bath, or a disused septic tank in which to hide. The sign of the Kings's Head had been moved from its place outside the bar - he couldn't remember when - and stuck on the wall a little higher and to the left of the Pensioners' Corner cheque. The King looked a bit like Henry the Eighth - typically Rhodesian - a belligerent warning behind the jovial cheeks.

The bar was packed with colonial memorabilia: two halberds at rest below a yard of ale; a tarnished brass post-horn curled into itself; framed prints of scenes from old Windsor, including the Bell of Ouzely behind cracked glass; a number of fine mirrors advertising fine liquors: John Haig - Scotch whisky - Quality with age; Kingston rum - Jamaica; Newcastle - Brown ale; Black and White...

"Same again, Sir?"

Dutch Willy nodded coyly to the friendly barman, said "Yes please", and fumbled in his safari suit pocket for yet another hundred dollar note. Remember when a beer cost one and thruppence... no more after this... don't want to arrive drunk at the holding cell... Jesus, how did I get a paunch so suddenly... er... "Thank you."

"You're welcome."

"The President is an arsehole."

"Sorry?"

He'd have to shout in order to be heard above the din. "THE PRESIDENT IS AN ARSEHOLE!"

A Man with a bullet-shaped head and dark glasses the colour of a Milk of Magnesia bottle pushed his way through the crowd and thrust his face to within an inch of Dutch Willy's. "What did you say?"

His breath smelt of boiled cow intestines.

"I said... I said the... er... President is a... er... an arsehole."

Dutch Willy's beer went flying out of his hand and his face came crashing down on the Rhodesian teak counter where it collided with an ashtray, which advertised Dunhill cigarettes. Then he was waltzed around a bit before being flung against a mirror, which advertised James Grafton and Son - Gunsmiths to the Gentry - Bond St London. Finally, barely conscious, he came to rest eyeball to eyeball with a Scottish piper in full regalia, playing, according to the lyrics printed below his kilt, "Amazing Grace".

As he drifted in and out of consciousness he thought he heard applause, and he wondered why. Then he heard rain pounding a tin roof. Then he felt rain. Or was it a shower? Too warm, surely, for rain. Then he became fully awake and got a worm's eye view of several flexible penises connected to several pairs of inflexible dark glasses, splashing piss on his head. He made a cry deep down in his throat, and he tried to sit up. The bar had gone silent except for a few disapproving clicks from patrons: witnesses yet again to somewhat unorthodox legal procedures.

He was jerked onto his feet. A powerful hand grabbed the thinning hair on his head and forced him to look at a kind of honours board on the wall behind the bar. It was a chronicle of all the men, over the years, who had thrown five aces. It ranged from 1975 to 1989. A voice, menacing, attached to the hand, said: "What is that, you white scum?"

Dutch Willy, doing his best to keep drops of urine out of his mouth, sounded as if he was blowing out birthday candles.

"Speak, you gay gangster! We know that those are names of Selous (he pronounced it Selouse) Scouts, but we want to hear it from you." The hand shook his head, which excited the remaining drops of urine, and he blew out candles so hard that he began to hyperventilate. "Speak, Blair's boy, speak!"

At last he managed to say: "Looks like one of the more eventful occurrences of 1980 was G. Harvey throwing five aces three times...."

He regained consciousness for the second time that night when the stench of human ordure acted upon him like smelling salts. He had achieved his aim. He was in a holding cell. He awoke in a standing position with bodies closely packed around him. He was the only white person among the thirty or so inmates in a room that was originally intended to accommodate a maximum of eight. His head ached, his chest ached, his entire body ached. He realised with alarm that he was barefoot. His watch was missing; so was his cash and, oh no! his lucky

134

rabbit's foot. In return he found himself the proud possessor of a small tin bucket, a portable lavatory.

The men closest to him saw that he had come awake, and they clicked their tongues in sympathy. They said they were sorry, and one old man gave him a worn pair of orange and yellow slip-slops to put on his feet. In the terrible days that followed he was to learn the true value of Zimbabwe's most familiar footwear, after the tackie.

It was time for the prisoners to sleep. The policeman on duty arranged them in such a way that each one could stretch out full length as long as he remained on his side and as long as he didn't mind someone's face in the back of his head and someone's head in his face, and someone's bucket poking into something somewhere. Even more than his aching head, Dutch Willy was conscious of his belly cushioning a bony spine. Every half hour, when circulation began to play up, the prisoners were commanded to get to their feet, stand for a minute, and then lie down on their other sides. The stench of diarrhoea was almost unbearable - a truly effective appetite suppressant.

When morning finally arrived and the cell became partly illuminated by leaking sunbeams, Dutch Willy realised that he was in desperate need to relieve himself of a pint or so of detoxified Castle lager. He struggled to his knees, undid the fly of his safari-suit shorts, and positioned the bucket. He waited for the piss to flow, but nothing would come. His bladder was aching with pressure - but nothing would come. He shut his eyes tightly and forced himself to think about the weight he was going to lose. But nothing would come. He must find a more private place. Adjoining the cell was an ablution area where he could detect no groaning sleepers. He had to step over a dozen bodies to get there but he was desperate. The stench seemed to be seeping into his brain. And it got stronger as he approached a lavatory bowl supporting a pyramid of shit; and shit and other kinds of less identifiable discharge all over the floor. He quietly blessed the old man for the pair of slip-slops as he slipped through the slops looking for a private place to pee. The shower cubicle was ankle deep in excrement; the wash basin was full of greenish vomit; only one of the water taps worked - at a trickle. No doubt about it, Dutch Willy was going to lose weight.

He began the process, leaning against the wall with his back to the other prisoners, by releasing a pint or so of liquid from his aching bladder into the superfluous bucket. The process continued when he refused to eat breakfast, which consisted of a large enamel dish of mealy meal porridge placed on the floor in the middle of the cell. The prisoners dug in with their diarrhoea-stained hands. The process climaxed when, a week later, he was brought before a magistrate who referred him to a judge who sentenced him to death for treason. The sentence was commuted to forty years hard labour, and when I visited Dutch Willy at Khami Maximum Security prison, the day before yesterday, I noticed that the process had been partially successful. He was as thin as a rake, but his paunch - his Rhodesian Front - had refused to capitulate and was, by contrast, larger than ever.

THE WORKSHOP

It was after attending his umpteenth workshop that Goodlord Mararira decided the time was ripe in post-independent Zimbabwe to run a workshop about how to run a workshop. He spent weeks pouring over American best sellers, which used key words and phrases like "proactive", "synergy", "win/win", "downsize", and "paradigm shifts". Excessive usage, he decided, would finally unlock the meanings of these "unAfrican" terms.

He chose, as his target audience, representatives of various youth brigades, women's groups, affirmative action societies, and the "budding writers" of Bulawayo. He thought about inviting some war veterans but his courage failed him. He chose a venue, which supplied starched white tablecloths, lashings of Mazoe orange juice, and a portrait of His Excellency the President and First Secretary of the Republic of Zimbabwe. He power-dressed for the occasion by wearing a powder-blue safari suit with no fewer than seven pens in the left pocket of his safari-suit shirt, and a large, barely used handkerchief in the right pocket of his safari-suit shorts. He drew the line at veldskoens, opting for his abundantly laced North Stars.

He agonized about a topic for the workshop, something fresh and stimulating. He finally settled on "Black Racism: Contradiction or Paradox?" Even though he urged the participants to be proactive, to synergize, to create a win/win situation, to downsize if necessary, and to take cognizance of paradigm shifts, the workshop on how to run a workshop was a flop. The youth brigaders (all of whom were over the age of forty) claimed that the topic was racist; women's groupers kept breaking into song; the affirmative actioners wanted to take over the venue (since it was owned by whites) and convert it into an office for themselves; and the budding writers wrote protest poems - in free verse - all over the starched white tablecloths.

It was back to the drawing board for Goodlord. The way forward, he realized, was to run a workshop about how to run a workshop. He chose as his target audience representatives of the Bulawayo Residents Association, Burial Societies, NGOs, and Gracious Ladies. He thought about inviting some war veterans but, once again, his courage failed him. He decided against a provocative topic, this time, and settled on "White Racism: Tautology or Redundancy?" He chose an out-of-town venue: a Safari lodge whose operator had run out of American, German and Spanish speaking clients, and who was therefore prepared to accept local currency. The lodge provided animal skin mats, lashings of Mazoe lime juice, and a portrait of the elephant hunter, Frederick Courtney Selous. He decided to dress moderately for the occasion and wore his beige safari-suit, with only two pens - albeit Parkers - in his shirt pocket, and no handkerchief in his shorts pocket. He thought his North Stars would not be out of line.

The workshop seemed to be going well - fifteen bottles of Mazoe lime juice had been consumed - when one of the participants observed that whites who were not racists were more racist than whites who were racist, since they obliged blacks to approve of them or, at the least, not hate them very much. Was this, the participant wondered, tautology, or was it redundancy; or couldn't it perhaps be a bit of both? Whereupon another participant accused the speaker of shifting paradigms; another urged the speaker to be more proactive; yet another called for a win/win situation; Goodlord himself reminded everyone to be synergistic even if it meant downsizing the discussion groups. But it was no use. Chaos ensued. The Bulawayo Residents Association accused the city council of being more attentive to potholes in the low density suburbs than potholes in the high density suburbs; The Burial Society members called for cheaper coffins; the NGOs were too busy deciding which of the indigenous participants they would later be able to screw or be screwed by; and the Gracious Ladies kept breaking into song. The workshop on how to run a workshop on how to run a workshop was another flop.

He decided to give it one last go. He invited the Aloe Society, the German Shepherd Club, the Home Brewers Club, and residents from the Edith Duly Home for the aged. He chose as a topic, "The role of Algae in Ponds, Swimming Pools, and Drinking Water". He decided to dress ethnically and wore a brightly coloured soutane, which he borrowed from a Ghanaian friend called Kofee. The venue was the home of the Chairlady of the German Shepherd Club, somewhere in Burnside. They used the lounge with its comfortable sofas and settees, pouffes, and rocking chairs. The hostess laid on plenty of gin and tonic, sherry, and spiced wine.

Before Goodlord could introduce his keywords and phrases, a member of the Home Brewers Club called for drinks all round, disappeared into the garden, and returned with two dozen quarts of home-brewed dark ale. The German Shepherd Club drank gin and tonic, the aged from Edith Duly drank sherry, the Aloe Society drank spiced wine, and the Home Brewers Club drank beer. Goodlord drank something of each, and before he knew it he was harmonizing to a song called "Roamin'in the Gloamin'". Much later that night, when the last of the participants had straggled off home and Goodlord, with his arm around the Chairman of the Home Brewers Club, was beginning to master the tune and lyrics of "Lily of Laguna", it dimly occurred to him that his workshop about how to run a workshop about how to run

139

a workshop about how to run a workshop had been a resounding success – and he never once had to use the key words.

THE VICTIM

The Officer in Charge

After a tip-off by the public at large we proceeded to the bush there by Circular Drive. We found the body hanging from a tree. He was using a leather belt. Yes, he was naked, and it is true what you say, but those who laughed, they were seriously reprimanded.

We unhooked the belt, put the body in a plastic, and took it to the Mpilo mortuary for identification. Yes, too full. You wouldn't believe. We had to leave it there on the ground. Then we were looking for someone to identify the body. Ja. Terrible.

Constable M......

We could not help it, to laugh. His penis was erect. Like this.

Constable N.......

No, we didn't remove the belt. Because that is not our job. All what we did is our job.

The Victim's Brother

When the police came and told me, I was very sad. My sister, she cried, but I did not cry. Only when I saw my brother - the oldest boy - lying there with no clothes and with his belt, which was my father's, who is now late... his belt....

Yes, my mother is also late. Now it is just me and my young sister. My uncle sends us money from South Africa. I change it with Vapostori... is why my brother went to jail. The police catch him changing forex with Vapostori. Fourth Street.

I had to undo the belt. It was too tight. I could not look at him. I cried all the time. Yes, they did. They found his clothes in the bush and gave them to me.

The Victim's Sister

When they released him he looked terrible. His skin was like ash. He wouldn't look at us or even talk to us. Mostly he lay on his bed. He cried quietly, sometimes, all night. No, he wouldn't eat a thing. Not even chicken. He just lay there.

His girl friend did not even know he was out of jail. His friends. Nobody.

Yes, he was in a lot of pain. I think his bottom was very sore. He wouldn't let us help him. He turned away from us. He used to be such a happy boy - always laughing and joking. Lots of girls.

The Prison Officer

Yes, it is officially forbidden to lock up children with adults, but we do it all the time. They pay us well and it makes them less aggressive. Sometimes it is very hard to control these people.

I do remember him, but it was not I who smuggled him from the juvenile block to the adult block. That was another officer. No, I can't do that. No, I don't feel bad. Why should I feel bad? He was exchanging money on the parallel market. He was unpatriotic. We are a sovereign country. We are tired....

The Rapist

142

I paid a lot of money for that "woman". All my forex. But I got it back in a few weeks by renting him out to the other prisoners. No, he was easy to hide in these overcrowded cells. And he was very small.

That is not true. He screamed a lot because of the sores, but how can you say he didn't like it when I can bring you witnesses to prove that he sometimes got an erection. Strewsgod. Like this.

WHITE MAN CRAWLING

It was to be a surprise – from those grateful commercial farmers aka safari operators who had managed to hold on to their most productive farms and so, continue living in the lifestyle to which they had been accustomed since Independence: a lifestyle which did not exclude annual holidays in Alpine ski resorts, house boats on Lake Kariba, shopping sprees, in private jets, to Sandton City, and best of all, jamborees in their iconic 4 x 4s.

The venue was one home of Nols Bosluis, a beautiful Cape Dutch affair (not Nols, the home!), which overlooked the Sebakwe river deep in the Zimbabwe Midlands. Before the so-called Land Reform programme Nols had owned seventeen farms, all but three of which he had since, in a spirit of patriotism and love of his fellow man (he would not admit to coercion), given to the government for purposes of re-settlement. They had duly been resettled, not by the peasants, but by the local honourable minister and his relatives. And that is the reason why Nols had been allowed to keep a few.

His son, Zuluboy, and his daughter Swazigirl, had been flown back for the occasion, from their exclusive schools in South Africa. Delightful children, they never spoke, not even when spoken to, because they had become chronic cell-phone users with over-developed thumbs. His fellow commercial farmers, those few remaining on the land because they had done the sensible thing – stay loyal to the ruling Party – were to contribute in their own humble ways. Bols would slaughter a hundred guinea fowl, Hols would shoot a kudu, Dols would de-stock the National Breweries, and Vols would use his fleet of vehicles to transport the VIPs including the guest of honour.

Their pretty wives (meaning the servants) would do the salads and the puddings.

Everybody except those few in the know took it for granted that the guest of honour would be the honourable minister. After all he had been so good to the remaining commercial aka white farmers. Hadn't he allowed them to sponsor his recent election campaign against those losers the MDC? Hadn't he condescended to receive from these patriotic sons of the more arable soil tankers of petrol and diesel, truckloads of maize meal and elephant meat, bowsers of opaque beer? And hadn't he, consequently, won the seat? But Nols had a surprise for his guests, a big – indeed an enormous – surprise!

Long after the guests had assembled at the Bosluises' Cape Dutch farmhouse, the honourable minister and his entourage arrived. Nols called out, "Greetings Comrade Honourable Minister; I have kept you a bottle of your favourite Scotch whisky, Chivas Regal."

"My friend, Nols," the honourable minister replied, "and I have brought you assurances from above that you may keep your remaining farms for the time being."

Then Nols, all six foot four of him, did an amazing thing. He performed a ritual that had not been witnessed since the days of King Lobengula. He walked on his knees, bottle of whisky held high, right across the front lawn of the house, to the honourable minister. His cartilages could be heard creaking (old rugby injuries) from as far away as the river front where crickets in their numbers began to accompany the sound. To rapturous applause, the honourable minister received his gift with noble condescension. Those guests who thought that this was the climax of the party were delightfully mistaken. What's that rattling sound in the distance? Are those riverside crickets on steroids? No, it's a helicopter, Vols's pride and joy, and it's bringing the real guest of honour. Men, women and children form a huge circle on the lawn, and the helicopter lands in the middle of it. Wind generated by the propeller blows deliciously in all directions discomposing hairdos and caftans, and threatening to trash Baby Bosluis's cole slaw. The helicopter disgorges… no it can't be! How did Nols manage it? You don't get much higher in the political hierarchy than this. It's not a name to be bandied about but we can tell you that the guest of honour appears to be a woman, with a voice like a trumpeter hornbill. For two hours, standing at the foot of the helicopter, flanked by half a dozen bodyguards, she trumpets on about the girl child, then about AIDS, then about operation Garikayi (she can't remember the Ndebele equivalent), then about, of all things, water pumps!

Where's Nols, by the way? What's he been doing during the speech? Where the heck is mine host? Arms and the man, we sing! He appears from the darkness with a bullock in tow, a large black bullock. He leads it to within metres of the trumpeter hornbill. Then, seemingly out of nowhere he draws a butcher's knife. The bodyguards feel for their weapons. The party is silent. Even the crickets down by the river have ceased their clamour. Then the ejaculations as Nols expertly kills the bullock and tears out its still pulsating heart. This he offers to the real guest of honour who politely declines and asks if she couldn't rather have a piece of Kentucky Fried Chicken with chips and tomato sauce.

WHITE MAN WALKING

He was striding down the pedestrian track between Ruskin Road and the Hillside School playing field. I was cycling in the other direction, on my way to Girls' College, which is situated in Suburbs. It was early, before the traffic build-up, so the road was pretty empty: one or two Townsend girls, their satchelled dresses riding up their back legs; a Milton boy with a crooked leg, taking his rest on the corner of Walpole Road; an old tramp with cataracts in his eyes, rummaging in dustbins for empty plastic bottles. And the ubiquitous pied crows.

It must have been late August because the bauhenia variegata - white, pink, and magenta - were in full flower; and from behind more than one ugly durawall wafted the sweet scent of buddleja. The mornings were still rather chilly so I was wearing my long-sleeved Rupert Bear jersey. He didn't seem to mind the cold since he wore only a thin khaki shirt with short sleeves rolled above his biceps, a tiny pair of faded blue rugby shorts, and veldskoens without socks or laces. He carried a walking stick, which looked more like a weapon in his hand. Slightly ahead of him, straining against a leather choker, was the biggest Staffordshire bull terrier I had ever seen. It was brindle in colour and it was the size of a ten gallon drum.

We exchanged glances: mine satirical, his contemptuous. I judged that he had recently retired and was learning to contend with empty hours, empty days, weeks, months.... Striding with his long, muscular legs, one slightly thinner and less muscular than the other: evidence of a rugby injury: snapped tendon perhaps, or torn cartilage. Wielding his stick rather than using it as a support. Searching the horizon, with half closed eyes, for challenges to his Old Boy vigour. Attached to the other knuckly hand, barely controlled, panting, eyes popping, was his correlate: an affectionate dog that liked nothing better than a good scrap with the wheel of a motor car slowing down.

Perhaps he had been sales manager for a spare parts factory; or senior representative for a company that built swimming pools; or chief security officer for a firm that specialized in burglar alarms. Perhaps he had been a school teacher like me. Perhaps he had been to Rhodes University in South Africa and majored in Geography and Physical Education, with Sociology, Social anthropology, and Bantu Law as fillers. I turned my head to look at him but he did not turn his head to look at me. He had a soldier's bearing; I slouched, even on my bicycle, like a lily, straining after light, that had grown too heavy for its stem.

When next we passed each other, more or less the same time the following day, we exchanged slightly altered glances: mine curious, his amused. His full crop of hair, I noticed, was cut in such a way as to give maximum exposure to his ears, the lobes of which resembled Brussels sprouts. Keloids. My hair was too long for my age, and for the age. Beatles style, it made me look a bit like John Lennon might have looked in middle age. His dog's pink tongue was foaming.

Our brief encounters went on for years, season after season. We shared the experience of cement durawalls going up and hibiscus hedges coming down. We shared the times with children dawdling to school, and domestic workers waiting outside locked gates; tramps and pied crows ransacking dustbins; the mingled suburban smells of floor polish, coal smoke, chrysanthemums, tomato plants, dog shit, and the exhaust fumes of cars that should long since have been taken off the road. And over the years our glances altered to looks of friendliness accompanied with smiles and nods. His dog, no longer straining ahead,

148

but lagging behind, greying muzzle, suppurating eyes, would recognize me and wag his stumpy tail.

Then, one day, he came alone, not wielding his walking stick but using it to support his damaged leg, which had been slowing him down, and bending him, by almost imperceptible degrees, through the years. No dog. I looked at him with sympathy and he looked at me, briefly, with embarrassment for his grief. The line of his jaw had begun folding into his neck. Like mine. Like mine, the skin around the muscles of his legs and arms had begun to loosen and sag. I notice for the first time that he was wearing stockings, and that his shoes were tightly laced.

School holidays came and went, and when I resumed my school routine, I noticed that he was not on the road. Day after day, no sign of him. The poinsettias were particularly grand that wintry season. I fantasized that he must once have adored scarlet lips like that: Rita Hayworth's in his case; Sylvia Plath's in mine.

He was my analogue, and I missed him.

It must have been a good two months later - the jacarandas were coming out - that I saw him again, and I was shocked at what I saw. The once challenging stride had been reduced to a shuffle. When he saw me he smiled sheepishly and tried to straighten his back, but only his dewlap reacted. He was streaming saliva, and his eyes were lusterless. But there he was, on the pedestrian track between Ruskin Road and the Hillside school playing field, shuffling along in slippers and pyjamas, and a cordless dressing gown.

And he was there the next day, and the next. And we smiled at each other and wordlessly acknowledged the beauty of the jacaranda blossom and, a month later, the flamboyants on Kipling Drive. When the harvester ants came out we looked at each other knowingly - a sign of rain. He used the point of his stick to poke gently at chongololos, to see if they would curl up (girls), or writhe on their backs (boys). Once, a passing crow crapped on his head and, for the first time we communicated with laughter, silent though it was.

The last time I saw him before I changed schools and therefore routes, a miniature fox terrier trotted at his heels, a mere puppy, and when it saw me on my bike it growled. He winked at me and shuffled on his way. Not so the dog. It charged at me and sank its little teeth into the back tyre of my bicycle. I screamed at it to let go, and I could have sworn I heard the old man chuckle.

WHO REALLY BUILT GREAT ZIMBABWE?

(After Jorge Luis Borges)

[The original letter is in the estate of Great Aunt Nora, along with an India rubber dildo preserved in talcum powder, and a signed copy of *The Well of Loneliness.* While we have ascertained that the book and the dildo were private possessions, it is almost certain that the letter, a fragment of which follows, was the creation of a mischievous South African organization, bent on sowing seeds of division between the black and white peoples of the then Rhodesia. Great Aunt Nora's twin brother belonged to one such despicable organization, and he is the likely author. The text is in English but one or two Afrikanerisms justify the conjecture that it was translated from the Afrikaans.]

...will now focus on one of the most shocking monuments to power in Africa. My example is politically correct because, contrary to popular belief, it was not built by black Africans.

This so-called monument is comparable to the pyramid of Gizah and Die Taal Monument in South Africa as a symbol of male dominated political power, power over people. When the king coughs, you cough. When the king his balls scratches [sic], you your balls scratch [sic].

One theory is that it was created by Phoenician gold traders; another, by the queen of Sheba; yet another, by the Mwenemutapa dynasty: one group of the Shona speaking peoples. None of these theories is remotely true.

Great Zimbabwe, as the ruins are now called, was built - or the bulk of it anyway, by the Rhodesian rugby squad. In order for them to achieve peak fitness for their game against the New Zealand All Blacks and the British Lions, they went into secret training at a camp seventeen miles south of Masvingo, (then called Fort Victoria).

Their coach chose this site for two reasons: steep kopjes [sic] to run up and down and millions of stones lying around for the players to carry around while they trained. His fitness programme was simple but effective. At a central point in the valley, the players were into groups divided [sic] and each group was given an area to run to. They had to run with a stone in each hand and deposit it when they reached their given area.

In this way the tight forwards built the Acropolis, the loose forwards built the elliptical building, and the three quarter line built the rest. I was told by a surviving member of that squad, who wishes not to be named, that the so-called conical tower, which his group built, was their idea of a "whopping jaloga", and that he, himself, had carved the so-called soap stone birds based on a condom he had once seen which was tipped with a hard rubber pineapple. I asked about the crocodile that rests below the bird, and his nostrils flared proudly when he explained that the space between the jaws of the reptile and the claws of the raptor signified the glans of the penis, the focus of masculine glory.

All peace-loving Zimbabweans will be relieved to know, at last, that the ruins called Great Zimbabwe are nothing more than a vulgar Rhodesian aberration, and are no longer to be feared, as they have for centuries been feared, along with Die Taal Monument and the Pyramid of Gizah, as shocking symbols of masculine ...

No more of the letter has been unearthed.

WHO WILL GUARD THE GUARDS?

Do not underestimate the guilt that runs through the veins of half-decent white people who, for decades, benefitted by the exploitation of black and brown people. But don't take advantage of their guilt too often, like my erstwhile friend, Assistant Inspector Takesure Mararike [not his real name], who robbed me of my Toshiba laptop, my soul.

One morning I heard a banging at my gate, and there was Takesure with his pretty young wife, Cleopatra. He was a radio technician with the Zimbabwe Republic Police, and he had recently been transferred from Gwanda. He needed temporary accommodation, until the Force found him a house, and he'd heard that my servant's quarters were vacant. Indeed they were; for good reason. They consisted of one cramped room, a toilet without a seat, a shower without hot water, and a grimy fireplace. These *kias*, as they were called, symbolise the contempt with which settler employers treated their indigenous domestic workers.

I said I was ashamed of the place but if he was desperate he was welcome to stay there, free of charge for as long as necessary. That very afternoon he moved in, with his wife and three little children. I asked him to go easy on the water and electricity, both scarce and expensive commodities in Bulawayo, but he could help himself to as much firewood as he needed. (It was only after they had left that I discovered his wife had sold my entire woodpile to passers by.)

The next day there was a knocking on my door and I ushered in Takesure, looking very smart in his police uniform. He told me, over a cup of tea, how tough things were these days of economic meltdown in Zimbabwe. He'd heard that telecommunication companies in New Zealand were keen to recruit radio technicians from African countries, and could I help him with enquiries. I sat him down next to my Toshiba Laptop and together we surfed the internet until we found some friendly and helpful New Zealand web sites. It looked as if there

153

were indeed jobs going for radio technicians. I helped Takesure create a neat résumé, and we used my email address to apply for a job through Telecom Human Resources.

A week later, Takesure and his family were gone and so were my Toshiba Laptop (my entire data base), my son's bicycle, 25 litres of petrol, my backpack, my torch, and a change of clothes, which included my colourful woven belt from Guatemala, the only one in town. The police would not touch the case, and passed me on to the C.I.D. who invited me for questioning the following day.

My immediate concern was to visit my internet server in order to download any emails that had accumulated since the theft. There was one from the Telecom Recruitment Team:

"Dear Takesure

A job opening matching your profile for a position of Help Kiwis get connected has just been posted in our Career Section. If you would like to apply..." etcetera. O the satire of circumstance!

The Chief Inspector wearing dark glasses in a dimly lit room, was sitting at his typewriter when he motioned me inside. Laboriously he took down my statement shaking his head, as if in denial, at the mention of my chief suspect. He assured me that they would do everything they could to recover my property, and when he stood up to shake my hand I thought I saw my Guatemala belt around his waist.

IN THE BEAUTY OF THE LILIES

April Day, who had been born in April, was about to buried in April. Eighty years, give or take her name, separated the month of birth from the month of death. The place, however, was not different. She lay in state in her bedroom, once her parents' bedroom, on the same bed she had been born. One person, a midwife, had witnessed her birth; no one had witnessed her death – unless you could call her tabby, Tabby, a person. The cassia trees that lined Cecil Avenue were in full, fruity yellow flower, their dense canopies providing a welcome shade for the endless procession of men, women and children who relied on their legs to take them from one locked gate to another; or from one gathering of white-robed vapostori to another; or from one cardboard box vendor to another.

Earlier that morning, shortly before April had closed her eyes forever, a choir of Heuglin's robins had held her fading attention; and in the darkling landscape of her mind she might have recalled their gorgeous orange plumage and distinctive white eye stripes. But that wasn't the only music she might have been listening to; for in the portable CD player next to her bedside table, the last track, 21, the most glorious tenor voice in recording history was bringing the 'Ingemisco' from Verdi's *Requiem* to an end. No, not Enrico Caruso (earth), not Beniamino Gigli (water), not Jussi Björling (air), not Franco Corelli (fire), but a combination of the four elements, a quintessence: Thulani Khumalo. He would cancel his final La Scala performance as Pinkerton in Puccini's *Madama Butterfly* in order to sing at Miss Day's funeral in Bulawayo.

Her room was sparsely furnished. Against the wall opposite her bed was a wardrobe in dark wood, with a tarnished full length mirror, which, right now, reflected Miss Day's shamelessly exposed nostrils and the wiry mole hair at the base of her chin. The whole exuded a whiff of cologne and mildewed shoes. On the window ledge stood a brass vase with no fewer than twelve different specimens of wild flowers poking out of its dented lip. These flowers had been gathered a few days before from the encroaching bush of Miss Day's yard situated in the suburb of Hillside. Next to the vase was a red Smythson (of Bond Street) note book, A5, which contained sketches and notes on many wild grasses and flowers. These grew in the vicinity of Bulawayo. The last entered sketch was labelled, *eragrostis cilianensis*, followed by the common name: 'stink lovegrass.' April Day had been an amateur botanist. Professionally, she had been a music teacher, the proud possessor (thanks to Grandfather O' Casey) of a Bechstein baby grand. In a framed black and white photograph hanging from the picture rail on the wall opposite the window, her only child smiled stiffly. That picture had been taken shortly before Piccolo had been kidnapped by his English father, Sergeant-Major Blushington. The child must have been about five years old. He was wearing a sailor suit. In his left hand was a miniature Union Jack, in his right a golliwog with staring eyes and fuzzy hair. The only other decoration on that wall was a large print, signed, of the great African American singer – that sweet rumble of thunder – Paul Robeson.

On the wall above her headboard was a framed print of a mural depicting John Brown as a flame-haired giant, arms stretched in the form of a cross, with a bible in his left hand and a rifle in his right. The middle ground depicts the clash of pro-slavery and anti-slavery forces. In the background there is a tornado squaring up to a raging inferno.

Miss Day chose the picture, not for its allegorical intent but because, she told Tabby, John Brown resembled her Irish grandfather, O'Casey. There was another, more sentimental, reason. The print is entitled: TRAGIC PRELUDE.

When April started teaching at White Rhino High, she was already way past retirement age; but music teachers were as scarce as hens' teeth in Bulawayo, so she was employed on a contract basis, one year at a time. She was grateful for the job because she had lost her life savings some years back when her bank bolted its doors.

One Sunday she and her friend and colleague, Clementine Ndimande, decided to go on a picnic in the Matobo communal lands some thirty kilometres south of Bulawayo. It was the last Sunday of the school holidays, promising to be fine and mild. Being January, in the middle of a fairly good rainy season, there should be wild flowers in bloom. Clementine, a maths teacher, was many years younger than April, in her fifties. She was a widow, and her three children, all with families of their own, were living in the Diaspora.

They packed a basket with cheese and tomato sandwiches, ginger snaps, and a thermos flask of sweet milky tea. They took the old Gwanda road in Clementine's yellow Datsun Sunny, and stopped along the way to visit Mzilikazi's memorial. He was known as the Lion of the North and he was the founder of the amaNdebele nation. He was a Khumalo.

The muted sound of a cow bell reached them and they continued on their way towards the eastern Matobo hills. They found a spot beside a stream, running quite strongly at this time of year. They selected and found a delicious patch of shade under a mobola plum tree, took out two folding chairs from the boot of the car, spread a checked tablecloth on the ground, and proceeded to unpack their

157

picnic. Almost immediately a yellow-billed kite appeared out of nowhere, settled itself on the topmost branch of a dead pod mahogany, and waited patiently for scraps. Clearly other picnickers had preceded April and Clementine to this lovely spot. Both women sighed with pleasure as they sank into their chairs and looked about them. The only cloud in the sky was a fading vapour trail connecting Bulawayo to Johannesburg. In the distance a Cape turtle dove kept repeating its three haunting notes. The friends munched happily on their sandwiches.

Presently a boy appeared, seemingly from nowhere. He was about twelve years old and he was wearing the uniform of a North American mission school run by the Church of Christ. He was incompletely dressed, however, for he wore no shoes and stocks, no cap, and no tie. He was covered in dust. The teachers from White Rhino High assumed he was going to beg from them, but they were wrong. He asked for a crust of bread to feed to the yellow-billed kite, which had taken to the air. 'Watch this,' he said in English. He launched the crust; the kite swooped and caught it just when gravity had begun to reverse its trajectory. April offered the boy a ginger snap but he politely declined. Then he said, 'Would you like to hear me sing?' The teachers said they would. He gave them a bright smile, and in the purest treble April had ever heard, he sang:

John Brown's body lies a-mouldering in the grave;
John Brown's body lies a-mouldering in the grave;
John Brown's body lies a-mouldering in the grave:
But his soul's marching on!

Glory, glory, hallelujah! Glory, glory, hallelujah!

158

Glory, glory, hallelujah! His soul's marching on!

April prompted him on the second stanza: 'He's gone to be a soldier in the army of the Lord...' and they sang it together through to the end.

April was enthralled. She asked the boy his name – Thulani. Would he like to sing before the school children at White Rhino High? Vigorous nodding. Once term started she would make arrangements. She would get in touch with senior staff at the mission school where Thulani was a boarder. He could spend a night or two with her or Mrs Ndimande, and she was sure her school would provide transport. The boy then said he wanted to show them something, and motioned them to follow him.

They walked along the stream a little way before following a cattle path towards a low-lying granite hill covered in yellow and orange lichen. In cracks where soil had gathered, ferns and mosses grew interspersed with aloes and resurrection plant. Brightly coloured rock lizards, camouflaged by the lichen, were sunning themselves everywhere. They were aware of being stared at by half-hidden dassies, elephant shrews, and leguaans.

April smelt them before she saw them. Just over the top of the hill, in a damp, sandy area to the right was what Thulani wanted to show them: a crowd, a host of vlei lilies, hundreds of them in full flower, white with pink keels. The combined sight and scent was breathtaking, overwhelming for April who burst into tears and spontaneously took the boy into her arms. 'My family is buried there,' said the boy.

'Your family?' She let go of him and stared into his eyes.

'My mother, my father, my uncle, and my two sisters.'

159

'What happened?'

'Soldiers.'

'Soldiers?'

'Soldiers with red hats. I was away at the mission. Our neighbour told me. The soldiers said my uncle was a dissident, and because he was living with us we were also dissidents. They locked all of them in a hut and set fire to it.'

April and Clementine looked at each other helplessly. Then they looked back at the field of lilies, beginning to sway in a sudden gust of warm air. They offered their condolences and promised the boy they would not forget him. It was with heavy hearts that they returned to Bulawayo, and prepared to face the new school year.

Not only did April manage to persuade her school to invite Thulani to perform at Monday assembly, but she persuaded the Board of Trustees to award him a music scholarship, which included tuition in all subjects. He was to board with Mrs Ndimande while April would see to his voice training. The Church of Christ saw the move as beneficial to the child, especially since he was an orphan, so they gave the move their blessing.

At his first assembly performance, Thulani did not sing 'John Brown's Body', he sang 'Hear My Prayer', and he learnt it by listening over and over again to Miss Day's 1927 recording by the famous boy soprano, Ernest Lough. That morning, in the school hall, with more than 700 girls and boys in attendance, you could have heard a pin drop. The entire school was stunned by the ineffable beauty of Thulani's voice. He was soon in great demand, not just at school functions, but at weddings, funerals, and baptisms. He flourished in the foster care of his two mothers, and a community that appreciated his gift.

The treble is a short-lived range. A year after attending White Rhino High, Thulani's voice began to break, and his music teacher became very apprehensive about the future. Nevertheless she continued to coach him, insisting in particular on breath control. Teacher and student adapted to a lower, more limited range. In Miss Day's experience, pre-pubertal boys with treble voices tended to become baritones or basses, while those with alto voices tended to become tenors. When the adolescent voice began to seal its cracks, about a year after the first signs of breaking, it became clear to April that Thulani, against expectation, was becoming a tenor. He had a natural ability to blend head and chest notes, and it wasn't long before he could produce a high C and then a high D, with a timbre that reminded April of a warm blade passing through butter. She also taught him to play the piano to the level of Grade 8, with the Royal Schools of Music in London.

Thulani stayed on at White Rhino High until he had completed his A Levels. Then, with Miss Day's support, he found a place at a university in South Africa where he majored in voice and piano. Gradually they began to lose touch with each other; but the less April heard from her protégé in person, the more she began to hear about him in public. He got his first solo role with the Cape Town Opera company, as Rodolfo in Puccini's *La Bohème*. It wasn't long before he was touring the great opera houses of the world, increasing his repertoire, accommodating his flexible voice to lyric, *spinto*, and dramatic roles. Like Caruso, he could sing light bass roles; like Gedda he could hit the high F note in Bellini's 'Credeasi Misera' without whistling. After ten years on the circuit he was being universally acclaimed as the greatest tenor in recording history.

When he heard from an old school friend that Miss Day had died, he dropped all his appointments and caught the earliest flight home to Bulawayo. The funeral service was to take place at the crematorium the following day. Clementine Ndimande had made all the arrangements. She was thrilled when her foster child phoned her from the Oliver Tambo airport in Johannesburg to say that he would attend the funeral service and would like to sing for his departed music teacher. He also begged her to take him to his family home in the Matobo Hills. There was something he needed to do.

Clementine was at the Bulawayo airport to meet Thulani. She had driven there in her yellow Datsun Sunny so that they could go straight out to the communal lands. They hugged each other speechlessly, and there were tears, not only from the old school teacher's eyes. Clementine had packed a picnic lunch of cheese and tomato sandwiches, ginger snaps, and sweet milky tea. They said very little to each other on the drive out. The corrugations on the old Gwanda road were worse than ever but nothing much else had changed. When they passed the Mzilikazi memorial Thulani breathed, 'My ancestor.' Mrs Ndimande squeezed his hand.

They arrived at the old picnic spot and Thulani, after a quick snack, said he wanted to see if there were any lilies in bloom. It was unlikely this late in the season. He left Clementine under the mobola plum while he made his way to the granite hill. Before reaching the summit, he picked up the characteristic scent, and his heart began to pound. There was one umbel left in flower, one which grew on the mass grave of his family. Thulani gave thanks to his ancestors, plucked the umbel, which sprouted four flowers, and returned with it to the picnic spot. 'It's for Miss Day,' he said.

There were about forty people at the funeral service, all teachers and pupils from White Rhino High. It was a secular service. Clementine read a poem, and three of the pupils read tributes. Thulani placed the slightly wilted vlei lily on Miss Day's coffin, and then cleared his thoat to sing. The congregation were expecting 'Ave Maria' or 'Panis Angelicus' or 'Agnus Dei', but they got the tune of 'John Brown's Body' sung to the words of 'Battle Hymn of the Republic'. They all agreed that it was a stirring send off for the ancient music teacher, and that Thulani Khumalo had a lovely voice for that kind of singing.

TOMATO STAKES

*C*atha edulis or Bushman's tea, as it is known locally, possesses nothing like the stimulation of its northern relative, khat. Nevertheless, when the young leaves and shoots are infused in boiling water, it makes a refreshing drink. The Ndebele people do not call it *inandinandi* for nothing. When Lofty Pienaar was driven off his Umgusa farm by the Deputy Director of Prison Services (who graciously let him keep his house and 10 hectares of land) he made a decision, after consulting his foreman of 20 years, Tobias Banda, to go into commercial production of this small indigenous tree.

Lofty Pienaar had been at boarding school with me in the 60s. His father worked at the Thornwood asbestos mine just outside Gwanda. My father worked at the Lannenhurst asbestos mine just outside West Nicholson. So we had something in common – fathers who would probably die of asbestosis. On our way to and from school, we shared a compartment (with other boarders) in the steam train that huffed and puffed between Bulawayo and the South-Western districts, and we shared a fascination for the bush. Every Sunday, after church, we would bunk out of the hostel and head for the little patch of wilderness that flourished between our school and the race course. There we would trap mice, shoot small creatures (with our catapults), and raid birds' nests for our burgeoning egg collection. The mice we would skin, hoarding the pelts until we had enough –hundreds – to make a kaross. We used coarse salt to preserve the tiny pelts and to flavour the birds, usually mossies, which we sometimes managed to shoot, then pluck, gut, and cook over surreptitious fires.

After school we went our different ways, I into social work, Lofty into farming. He had been trained at Gwebi Agricultural College near Harare, and he was working as an assistant foreman on a tobacco farm somewhere in Mashonaland when he was called up, as I was, and all white men between the ages of 18 and 60, to help keep the Rhodesian Front in power. The next time I met him was at Vila Salazar on the Mozambique border. It turned out that we had both been posted to Sixth Battalion as B grade riflemen, which meant, mostly, digging bunkers and pit latrines. It was during an ambush deep in the Gonarezu Game Reserve, before we were ordered to "Shut the fuck up", that Lofty confided to me his dream of one day farming his own land.

That day came, ironically, after Independence. The sudden departure of thousands of white people, including landowners, meant that certain farms could be purchased for a song. With help from his parents and his older sister, then living in the U.S.A., Lofty put down the deposit on 350 hectares of prime land on the Umgusa River, near enough to Bulawayo for a market gardening project. A condition of his purchase was that he kept on the existing workforce of twenty men and women who lived with their families in a compound on the farm. The head of this workforce was an elderly master farmer called Tobias Banda, respectfully known to all as *Baba*, or Father.

As soon as he received his letter of No Interest from the new government, Lofty, with the help of his loyal workforce, set about transforming what amounted to not much more than a weekend family getaway (the previous owner had been a doctor with a practice in town) into a highly productive industry. In no time he began to supply Bulawayo, and then the entire country, with rich thick cream from his small herd of Jersey cows, the finest wool from his Angora rabbits, and,

165

from his irrigated market garden, artichokes, garlic, lettuce, potatoes, pimentos, and bean sprouts. He also became a major supplier of honey, and jellies made from wild fruits such as marula, kei apple, and *uzagogwane*.

As the years passed, Lofty Pienaar metamorphosed into a wealthy commercial farmer with all the trappings which that status insisted upon: a Mercedes Benz, a house boat on Kariba, a wife and four children, and a place on the Board of at least one private school. Once a year, usually during the Easter Break, we would get together –biltong and beer – and reminisce about the bad old days. Then the farm invasions began, the so-called Third *Chimurenga*. The first invaders were disgruntled war veterans and unemployed youths. They terrorised Lofty's workers by calling them *mtengesi*, and threatening to cut their throats. They were often drunk or high on *mbanje*; they carried axes and *knobkerries*; they banged tin cans and dustbin lids, shouted slogans, and sang songs of liberation.

By the time the second invaders arrived Lofty's workforce had been reduced to one, the elderly Tobias Banda. The compound had been burned to the ground, families dumped on the verges of the road to Victoria Falls. The second wave of invaders were rifle wielding policemen hired by the Deputy Director of Prison Services, who accompanied them waving a letter from someone very high up in the Ministry of Agriculture. This letter gave him the right to take over Lofty's farm. The Pienaars were given 24 hours to vacate the property or suffer arrest and imprisonment. But when the Deputy Director of Prison Services, after a cursory tour, decided that there were not sufficient power points in the house to service his daughters' computers, his son's play station, and his wife's DVD, not to mention the other three television sets, he graciously allowed Lofty to keep the

166

house – for the time being – as well as surrounding land amounting to 10 hectares or so.

The original invaders, who had transformed Lofty's market garden into a failed mealie field (someone had stolen the irrigation pump), but who were making quite a good living selling firewood and bush meat, at first welcomed the arrival of the police believing that they were there on behalf of them. Up until then, Lofty had managed to appease the ex-combatants (a number of whom would have been mere twinkles in their mothers' eyes on Independence Day) by giving them a Jersey cow to eat once a month. Their smoke-stained eyeballs widened in shock and indignation when the policemen's rifle barrels swivelled away from the Pienaar family and rested on them. They were ordered to vacate the farm immediately. Several shots were fired into the air to show that the Deputy Director meant business. Such are the vicissitudes of living history.

The leaves and bark of Catha edulis contain chemicals, which have a stimulating effect on the nervous system, similar to amphetamines, but The Voortrekkers, and long before them the aboriginal peoples of Southern Africa, used it as a treatment for chest complaints and influenza. All four of Lofty's children had suffered from croup, and it was Tobias Banda who had brought them relief by making them inhale the steam from boiling fresh *inandinandi* leaves. The old man knew where to find the small, evergreen trees with their drooping branches and pretty, serrated leaves. He and Lofty scoured Brachystegia woods and rocky hillsides in the Communal lands surrounding Bulawayo district; and they collected seeds by the thousand, which they planted and germinated in individual black plastic bags. Lofty did some research, and calculated that they would reap their first crop of leaves after seven or eight years of growth. Meanwhile he sold his assets, piecemeal, to keep food on the table and his children at school.

Five years later, Lofty's first batch of trees was looking good. Their pale grey, slender trunks were straight and true, their shimmering canopies already resembling the Australian blue gum. Meanwhile, the Deputy Director's 340 hectares had become completely deforested. From horizon to horizon not a single tree, not a single shrub, could be seen. It had all gone into firewood. Time for another cash crop. Tomatoes. Why not? But tomatoes need stakes, and the only stakes left on the Deputy Director's farm were the two that held up his washing line. He called in his erstwhile tree fellers and, looking meaningfully at Lofty's property, offered them 5 cents for every stake that they delivered to his door. The very next day he found himself happily possessed of 1000 tomato stakes, and Lofty Pienaar was ruined.

The day he hanged himself, from the lintel above the front door of his house, was the same day that Tobias Banda was found murdered in his hut, the word BLANTYRE carved on his chest. The war veterans were back, reinforced by army deserters, some waving AK-47s, others fondling hand grenades with rusty pins. In their wake, in permanent second gear, growled a silver Toyota Land Cruiser Prado VX Turbo Diesel 4x4 with bull bars, and all the mod cons including mp3, electric windows. Air bags, and a place to hold a can of coke. (The driver cannot be named but I can tell you that she inhabits the very largest 'small house' in Bulawayo, a pseudo-Tuscan style mansion boating no fewer than 30 en-suite bedrooms. I can also tell you that she flies to Dubai once a month to shop for clothes, handbags, shoes, and Kentucky Fried Chicken with chips and tomato sauce.)

She had hired the *toy-toying* mob in front of her to evict the Deputy Director of Prison Services from his farm. The podgy fingers of her bangled arm were waving a letter with a stamp from the office of the most powerful ministry in the land. She wanted this farm for her younger sister. She had already provided for her two brothers, all her surviving uncles and aunts, and both her unofficial lovers. One way or the other, she owned – for the time being – half of Matabeleland, nearly all of it deforested.

What happened to Lofty's family? They moved in with me. We are in the long and tedious process of emigrating to New Zealand where social workers are in short supply. Pam is a state registered nurse so she won't have any trouble getting employment. Lofty's blatant suicide and the grisly murder of Tobias have severely traumatised all of the children, especially little Theuns, the *laat lammetjie*. They have been going to counselling with a highly regarded NGO. Time will tell. Me, I have mixed feelings about leaving the land of my birth. I am a fourth generation European-African. Lofty was a 350-year European-African. So what! We plan to scatter his ashes on a windy day, one that would have made his family's Beta Mine house flap.

DEMOCRACY AT WORK AND AT PLAY

The Reverend Benati Jojova was thrilled that he would be playing an active role in Zimbabwe's constitution-making process. He had been invited to join an outreach programme in Gulati, not far from Bulawayo. Since he lived in Masvingo, and there were several outreach programmes in that district, he was a little puzzled as to why the organizers had decided to send him to Bulawayo, considering travel and accommodation expenses. Never mind. What an adventure! And what a feather in Zimbabwe's cap! It took the West... how long?- a thousand years to achieve democracy, and here we are, a little over thirty years old – our Lord's age on earth – poised to achieve government by the people, of the people... er... darn those English prepositions... to?... with?... over? Never mind.

His wife, Mai Queeny, had packed his suitcase with a spare dog collar and clothes for three days at the Heaven on Earth Guest House, where he would be boarding with four other outreach members, none of them, as it turned out, from Bulawayo, but all devout Christians. Their transport was an almost new Nissan Hardbody double cab, which had been seconded to Copac by a Masvingo member of parliament. The United Nations was footing the bill so there were no unseemly arguments about the exorbitant rental.

They waited arm in arm outside the rectory, for their colleagues to arrive. Mai Queeny had made her husband a thermos flask of oxtail soup, and packed him some peanut butter sandwiches for the road. "Don't forget to take your pills," she reminded him, and then, jokingly, "beware of izintombi! You know the reputation those Bulawayo girls have!" She gave his arm a loving squeeze.

170

"Nyarara, woman!" Benati chuckled. "I'm an old man – of the cloth. My hanky panky days are well and truly over."

"Then why does your Bible always open on the 'Song of Solomon'?"

"Ah… 'Thy lips, O my spouse, drop as the honeycomb: honey and milk are under thy tongue; and the smell of thy garments is like the smell of Lebanon'." That's where Yvonne got the title of her novel."

"You and half the world are in love with Yvonne Vera. Now you are going to pay homage to her in the city she so loved. I am a little jealous, you know."

The Reverend Jojova regarded himself as something of an authority on Zimbabwean literature, in particular Yvonne Vera, who had been the subject of his Master's thesis: *Beautifying the Horror: Biblical influences in the Writings of Yvonne Vera.* According to him, the cross, with its associations of extreme violence and ineffable beauty, was the central trope of all her writings. "More than that, my dear, I'll be entering the physical world of her greatest novel, *The Stone Virgins…*"

"You leave those virgins alone, wanzwa?"

They were both chuckling away when the transport arrived. Benate was the last passenger. His wife lifted his suitcase into the open back of the truck while he climbed into the last remaining space in the passenger seat. Greetings were made all round – these eminent persons of Masvingo knew each other - then farewells, and off they veered in the direction of Bulawayo. Apart from the multiple police road blocks (where smallish bills exchanged hands) it was a most pleasant journey. Padkos was shared as convivially as the conversation, which, naturally, focussed on the constitution-making process. All agreed that the current mutilated Lancaster House Constitution had to go, and there was some friendly dissent about the pros and cons of the Kariba draft, the NCA draft, and even the rejected Chidyausiku Constitution.

By the time they had located the Heaven on Earth guest house in one of Bulawayo's leafier suburbs, the sun had dipped below the horizon, and the sky – how did Yvonne Vera put it? – *that low you could lick it* – full of dust and wood smoke (in the windy month of August) – was glowing orange. They were warmly welcomed by their gracious hostess, Inkosikazi 'Vuvuzela' Bhebe (her nickname derived from the fact that she delighted in sprinkling talcum powder on her carpets, and sometimes on her guests), and shown to their rooms: prettily thatched rondawels. After unpacking and washing, the outreach team were treated to a delicious supper of fried chicken and rice followed by Vuvuzela's speciality: amasi with fresh fruit. They retired early in order to be fresh for the next day's trip to Tokwe School in Gulati communal lands. Before the power cut out, Benate read avidly, not from his Bible but from his dog-eared copy of *The Stone Virgins*. He was fascinated by the character, Sibasa, who could cavort with the body of a woman he had just decapitated and then, shortly after, rape and mutilate the sister, who must have witnessed the *danse macabre*. All that gore! One thing puzzled him, however: on page 61, the words: "A knee lifts up to touch the bottom of her legs". Was Sibaso a dwarf?

Perhaps because it was close to the National Park, perhaps because of its mountainous, bushy terrain, which would have made it difficult for the North Korean built armoured cars to traverse, the Fifth Brigade kept their Gulati incursions to a minimum. Dissidents, on the other hand, thrived there. Notorious killers like "Fidel Castro", "Idi Amin", "Danger", and "Gayigusu" regularly travelled through the region, wreaking havoc. Benate wondered if Sibaso wasn't based on one of these real life monsters. Just north-east of Gulati lay Adam's Farm, a

Christian commune, where, at the behest of some local squatters (and who knows which Chef?) dissidents axed to death 16 people including women and children, and a baby.

The road (sometimes no more than a track) to Tokwe school was almost impassable in places. Thank goodness the Nissan Hardbody had four-wheel drive. Benate and the others were stunned by the beauty of the landscape, and imagined how easily fugitives could hide themselves in those lichen-spattered, cave-pocked granite hills. When they arrived at the venue they saw a gathering of about 200 locals, mainly elderly women and children. They were met by a contingent of uniformed policemen and half a dozen young and youngish men who claimed to be war veterans or war collaborators. The hairs stood up on the back of Benate's neck when he noticed that they were armed with branches and machetes.

The police spokesman welcomed the outreach team and wondered if any of them could speak Ndebele; if not one of the war veterans would translate for them. One of Benate's colleagues said they been instructed to speak in English, and what the locals couldn't understand, Reverend Jojova would render in halting Ndebele. The team's driver, a retired headmaster, would chair the meeting while the others observed and took notes. He rummaged in the back of the truck and brought out a loud hailer. He swiched it on, tested it, turned to the assembled crowd and addressed them: "Salibonani abantumnyama!"

"Yebo!" from about a dozen voices.

"Linjani?"

"Siyaphila!" from about half a dozen voices.

Then he proceeded in English – to introduce the outreach members and to explain their mission. As a country of democratic principles, Zimbabwe wanted to create a people-driven constitution, which protected the rights of every individual —"

"What about homosexuals?" Interrupted one of the war vets.

One of the few men in the crowd put up his hand. "Er… yes?"

"Homosexuals should be stoned to death in public." This received an enthusiastic response from the crowd. Some women began to ululate.

The retired headmaster shouted into his loud hailer: "Please may we leave questions and answers until I have completed my address?" Two hours later his address was completed. He then asked what the crowd in general expected from a constitution, which would be the supreme law of the land and would shape Zimbabwe's destiny.

An ancient woman put up her hand. "We want a king." Cheers and ululations.

Another hand went up; a very old woman. "Our youth must be more respectful. They should greet us properly. The girls must go down on their knees."

Benate and the others were busy making notes. The policemen stood by smiling while the war vets moved in among the crowds, tapping their weapons against their thighs. A third hand went up; an old woman. She spoke in the vernacular: "There should be a minimum age limit on when children could be raped. It is my request that in the new constitution girls should not be raped before they are 24 years."

An old man wearing a straw hat put up his hand. "We want strong laws that will ban women from wearing trousers. How can I propose to her if she looks like a man? Do you think I am a homosexual like Blair?" Applause and loud laughter.

"Yes," shouted another old man, "and mini-skirts should also be banned. These girls are asking to be rapped."

A slightly younger woman: "Our girls must be stopped from going to Kezi Business Centre where they are becoming prostitutes."

"There should be more stories like "Superman" on the wireless."

"Clinics should be free like in Rhodesia."

It went on like this until Benate stood up and asked them if they would be less er... personal for a while, and look at issues like devolution, the electorate, parliament etc. The first speaker, the one who had denounced homosexuals, put up is hand – he seemed to be in cahoots with the war veterans – "We should have a president for life." Stunned silence.

One of the war vets strutted up to the retired headmaster, jerked the loud hailer from his hand, and addressed the now restive crowd. "Those of you who disagree with a life president must point out your houses to me." He felt in his trousers pocket and brought out a box of matches. He shook the box. "Let us have a show of hands." Dead silence. No hands went up. The policemen stood by smiling. The war vet threw the loud hailer to the ground and turned to the outreach team, who were all on their feet. "You sell outs!" he snarled, "crawl back to your MDC masters in Masvingo and tell them we already have a constitution – it's called the Kariba Draft. Go, before I set your truck alight!"

With ashen faces the five important persons, all somewhat overweight, scrambled for their vehicle and drove away. When Benate looked back he saw the war vets climbing into the rear of the police bakkie, waving their branches and their machetes in triumph. They drove back to Bulawayo in dead silence.

Their woes were not over. They found their suitcases strewn outside the gates of the Heaven on Earth guest house. After ten minutes of hooting and ringing the bell, they heard the side gate

175

opening, and there stood Mrs Bhebe, arms akimbo, a furious expression on her face. "Your sponsors are refusing to pay me. Go before I set my dogs on you."

"We have a democratic right-"

"Go!"

The portly, middle-aged five, scrambled for their suitcases, piled them into the back of the truck, squeezed into the cab, and veered off in the direction of Masvingo. Fortunately there was enough money left to fill the tank of the MP's truck.

Back at the rectory, while dunking a rusk into strong, milky tea, Benate was soothed with words and fingers by the solicitous Queeny, who hinted of even better things to come, later, in their bedroom.

After the actualisation of Queeny's hints, while she slept, Benate lit a candle, and began to read – not his Bible but *The Stone Virgins*, and when he got to the sentence on page 69: "He throws her towards himself", he muttered, "Darn these English prepositions"; but then his postmodern training kicked in and his face broke into a broad smile. He wished Queeny were awake so that he could proclaim his insight. Of course! This is subversive writing. Yvonne is insinuating the alterity of the subaltern into governing epistemes, granting it textual amplitude. Indeed, she manifests a semiotic modality, which unsettles the Colonialist as well as the Nationalist space. It's time for me to do my PhD, and my working title... my working title... let's see...er... how about: *Democracy at Work and at Play: The Subversive Function of Faulty Grammar and Mixed Metaphors in the Writings of Yvonne Vera*. The Reverend Benate Jojova MA, smiled happily, closed his book, blew out the candle, snuggled against the warm expansive body of his good wife, and fell into a deep, untroubled sleep.

TRYPTICH

The heat was intense. It came hurtling down from the sun. It bounced off the barren sub-soil. It turned the air into breath. He paused to rinse his parched mouth. The water from his bottle was above blood temperature. In the distance he could make out the rocky hill where he would set up an observation post. Patrolling was unpopular with most of the troopers; it was arduous, walking for days on end, lugging up to 50 kilograms of equipment. There was seldom any action, not like Fireforce. The day before, his stick had accounted for two Charlie Tangos, somewhere in the Mtoko area. Now he was close to Mozambican territory, alone, with a radio, an FN rifle, 100 rounds, and three grenades. Their safety levers had been taped down. He carried water and rations for three days.

This was Cornwallis' first solo mission, and he relished it. No mocking jibes from the other "ouens" every time he took an interest in an insect or a bird or a wild flower. He fingered the cob of marijuana deep in the pocket of his camo-jacket, which he had looted from the body of one of the gooks they had slotted the day before. He was looking forward to the brew up and the smoke he would indulge in after making camp.

His OP overlooked a village and a known crossing point for ZANLA operatives. His first task, once he'd reached the hill, would be to search it for caves or overhangs, which might be harbouring the enemy. How did his mother, with her incessant quotes, put it - cave-keeping evils that obscurely sleep. Something like that. He recalled stories of how dangerous caves had been to the imperial forces and the settler volunteers during the 1896 rebellions. The Shona chiefs built their kraals on or close to rocky hills where caves, some of them extremely deep, provided places to hide, places to store goods, places for rituals, and places to ambush the enemy, as was the case with Lieutenant William E. Barnes during a raid on Gatsi's kraal. He poked his nose into the opening of a cave and was shot, point-blank, in the chest. The weapon was a so-called "family gun", a relic of the Napoleonic wars, which could be loaded with anything from bottle tops to telegraph wires.

A stink of formic acid rose up from the parched earth as predatory Matabele ants ran in all directions looking for beetles and chongololos to terminate with extreme prejudice. From a distance came the anxious call of a Jacobin cuckoo in search of a bulbul's nest. It was well into November but no sign of rain. Cornwallis returned his water bottle to its place on his belt, adjusted his Bergen, looked cautiously around for any sign of human life, and proceeded on his way.

As he approached the hill he slipped his rifle off his shoulder, released the safety catch, and brought it into firing position. He was startled by a family of dassies scurrying down from a cabbage tree, newly in leaf. The late afternoon sun was beginning to dip behind the highest point of the hill, a split granite boulder, which resembled a still-life of a loaf of bread. With a practised eye, the eighteen year old trooper searched for a cave, or a crevice wide enough to accommodate an emaciated floppy and his AK 47. He made his way around the entire perimeter of the hill, looking also for an easy ascent. His heart began to thump when he discovered a disguised pathway. He was no tracker but he soon discerned barefoot prints, and he followed these, higher and higher up the hill until, just below the precipice, he found a cave. Clusters of sumach beans, now covered in tiny yellowish flowers and the woody threads of last year's pods, would have concealed the entrance from below.

A dilemma presented itself to Cornwallis. The safest way to clear a cave would be to toss in a grenade, but that would alert the village to his presence. If he looked into the opening, he might end up like poor Lieutenant Barnes, with a hole through his chest. He decided to move as close to the side of the cave as possible, then wait and listen. He picked his way through the curious vegetation of granite: lichens in four colours, silver clubmoss, ferns, vellozia, and the dead-alive resurrection plant. At the lip of the cave, he squatted, listening for the slightest indication of life in that dark recess. He had about two more hours of daylight at his disposal.

When a flock of redwing starlings started making noisy preparations for bed, Cornwallis decided to investigate the cave. He removed his camo-jacket and hung it on the barrel-end of his rifle. He was going to test the waters, so to speak. He pushed it, at shoulder height, round the edge of the cave. Nothing happened. He jiggled it. Nothing. He shook it off the barrel, took a deep breath, and swung into the cave. It reeked of dassie urine. When his eyes got used to the gloom, Cornwallis noticed an alien object halfway in to the recess. It was pink and tiny – a knitted baby's bootie. His mind went back to the footprints on the pathway – small, bare feet. A young mother, perhaps, or a sibling tasked with playing mommy for the day. The cave was about six metres deep, with a roof that sloped down from bending height at the entrance to crawling height at the gloomy back, where the trooper noticed a large clay pot. He needed to investigate this, but what if it was a booby trap? What if the cave extended beyond the limit of his vision, a sudden left turn, say, where death might be huddling?

He checked his safety catch, pointed his rifle at the pot, and advanced. It was full of fresh water. There were no booby traps, no extensions to the cave, but the water pot was very suspicious. Cornwallis decided then and there to set up his OP, not overlooking the village and the ZANLA crossing point, but the pathway which led to the cave. He returned to the entrance, looked carefully around, picked up the croaking call of a purple-crested lourie, and the more distant clonk of a goat bell, and then broke off some twigs of resurrection plant in order to sweep away boot prints in the soft sift of the cave floor. "Soft sift" – didn't his mother have something to say about that?

By the time he had located a suitable OP – between slices of the granite loaf, the sun had set, but there was enough light to make camp. From his Bergen he dug out a little gas stove, a cigarette lighter, an aluminium pot and a rat pack. With the remaining water in his bottle, he started the sacred process of a brew up. While he waited for the water to boil he set about rolling himself a joint. This was the life. His site was reasonably flat, and there was enough organic matter lying around to make a not too uncomfortable bed upon the rock.

While he dined on a tin of Vienna sausages in baked beans, the moon rose bathing all the world in a lemon yellow light. Why did his mother persist in calling it a ghostly galleon? He wondered what his family were doing at that moment. Without a doubt his sister, Ladybird, would be swotting for her O-levels; indeed, she was in the middle of writing her finals. His mother would be talking to her kitchen utensils while preparing an impossible pie or a pudding delicious. And his father? Probably setting up claymores around isolated farm houses. Wearing his dark blue police reserve uniform. He had been proud of Cornwallis for joining the RLI – "they have the faces of boys but they fight like lions" - instead of the Territorial forces like most of the other school leavers. He kept urging his son to join the Selous Scouts or the SAS, but Cornwallis knew his limitations. The RLI had taken him on only because, in 1978, they were becoming so short of manpower. Still he hadn't let them down, and his Commander had hinted at promotion to lance corporal if he continued to prove himself during Fireforce operations. With his radio and his rifle close at hand, Cornwallis slid fully clothed into his light sleeping bag, turned onto his side, and quickly fell into a profound sleep.

He was awoken by a dawn chorus of warblers and chats and babblers. He used a handful of precious water to rinse his eyes, dug out his binoculars, and began his observation. The sun hadn't yet risen but the early light aided him sufficiently. The direct approach to the cave was thick with bush, so "visitors" would probably skirt the hill. In that case he wouldn't be able to see them till they had begun their ascent. He didn't expect any activity until much later in the day. Time for breakfast. He made himself a pot of tea and opened a can of pilchards in chilli sauce. He scooped out the mess with hard biscuits, and crunched happily away. A rustling sound momentarily startled him. It was an indignant leguaan whose territory he had invaded. There was a gathering of clouds on the reddening horizon, a faint promise of rain later in the day.

After draining his tea, he got up to relieve himself as far away from his camp as possible. This happened to be the place where he should have set up his OP. He was in mid spray when his keen eyes picked out three antlike figures moving slowly out of the village towards the hill. He finished his business and went to fetch his binoculars. He made himself as inconspicuous as possible, prone, raised slightly on his elbows, like a leguaan, and focussed his lenses. The ants metamorphosed into ravens, then baboons, then… his heart began to thump… terrorists. They were walking in single file, slowly, because the one at the back seemed to be wounded. He was dragging a leg. The other two were heavily armed. The leader had a rocket launcher over his left shoulder and a rifle in his right hand. Number two was lugging a machine gun, an RPG-2, and – Cornwallis made out – even at such a distance, two or three Chinese manufactured stick grenades dangling from his waist.

What he should have done was radio his commander and request backup, but Cornwallis saw an opportunity to become a hero, earn the Bronze Cross, perhaps. How proud Blossom would be! He leopard-crawled to his camp site, and prepared himself for battle. He put on his webbing, checked his magazines, removed the tape from the safety levers on his grenades, and pulled some two-by-four through the barrel of his FN. He returned to his binoculars and trained them on the approaching trio. The wounded man was now lagging quite far behind. Were they headed for the cave?

The sun was quite high and burning the back of the trooper's neck when the two armed men moved beyond the angle of his vision. The wounded man was close enough for Cornwallis to see that he was completely unarmed. His face was twisted in agony and he was using both hands to drag the useless limb. It looked like a thigh wound – the entire trouser leg was soaked in dark blood. Cornwallis hurried to the other side of the hill top but there was no sight, not yet, of the other two. He felt a slight panic in his bowels. He scanned every inch of ground within his vision. Nothing. He decided to return to the village side to see if he could follow the progress of the wounded man, but he was nowhere to be seen. He ordered himself not to panic, and was about to return to the cave side when he noticed an antlike figure emerging from one of the village huts. He re-focussed his binoculars: the ant metamorphosed into a raven, then a monkey, then... a girl, a young woman, bearing two loads, one on her head and one on her back.

He scuttled over to the cave side. If they were heading there he should be able to see them without the aid of binoculars. Soon he should be able to hear them. Eyes peeled, ears intent, rifle poised... he waited. Nothing. Perhaps the two armed men were already in the cave, waiting for their wounded comrade. Why didn't they help him? The bastards. Better check on the nanny.... She was on the same track as the terrorists, heading towards the hill. The load on her head was an aluminium pot; the load on her back was a baby. The bitch was going to feed them! In the cave.

He returned to his OP and was just in time to see the wounded man crawling towards the cave. So, the other two were already inside. His mild panic was restored to mounting excitement. He would wait until the arrival of the girl, give them a bit of time to tuck into their sadza and relish – that would relax their vigilance – and then obliterate them. An image of the coveted Bronze Cross swam into his ken (as his mother would put it); then one of his father, holding him in a tight embrace... son, you did me proud! He slipped the high explosive grenade into the right pocket of his camo-jacket, and the white phosphorus into the left pocket. Then he waited for the girl to enter his angle of vision.

She was wearing a dress so ragged, it wouldn't survive another wash. Around her neck dangled a string of lucky beans – a flash of red to enhance the mosaic of lichens under her feet. She was lugging the pot up the gentle incline, while her baby slept against her back. She looked very young. Cornwallis felt an incongruous surge of desire. She entered the cave. He waited for about five minutes and then, ever so stealthily, making no more noise than a monitor lizard, proceeded to move.

Near the lip of the cave, grenade at the ready, he sat on his haunches and listened. The baby was gurgling, and the girl was humming an ancient tune. The men were silent. Cornwallis regretted that an innocent victim would have to be sacrificed but this was war. How did his mother put it... when the blast of war blows in our ears, then imitate the action of the tiger. Something like that. Using his teeth, he removed the pin of the high explosive grenade, counted the required seconds, lobbed it into the cave, and dived for cover.

The explosion was deafening. Even more deafening was the silence that followed. Trooper Swinburne waited for the smoke to clear, then, FN at the ready, swung into the cave. The water pot was smashed. Lumps of stiff porridge were strewn all over the place. The wounded soldier was mangled. The girl was barely alive. Along with its pink booty, the baby had now lost the top of its head to shrapnel. Of the two heavily armed soldiers there was no sign. They would be well on their way to the Mozambican border.

She was staring at him, eyes like saucers. Gay maroon patterns, spreading, put some life into the fadedness of her dress. While she feebly groped for her baby, Cornwallis dropped his trousers and, after some difficulty, found what he wanted to find, well lubricated with seeping blood, and as he moved in and out of her gradually cooling body, he blubbered, "I'm sorry... I'm sorry... so sorry... so sorry...."

2

184

The madam was having her friends to tea. She had just rung the bell for more hot water, talking, talking, nineteen to the dozen. Nobuhle could hear every word from the kitchen.

"I can picture them now, those little tykes, arguing about whose turn it was for Blossom's leftovers. They used to wait by the gate... goodness, I'm a poet and yet I didn't know it... not the main gate... isn't that an example of assonance? But the little 'wicked wicket' gate... who can guess where I'm quoting from? Olga? You're the literary type. Come on, it's easy... no? Edwin Muir... or was it Blunden? Anyway... this shortbread is delicious, Mabel, thank you for bringing it... anyway, it was the one near the servant's quarters, and Blossom always came home through that gate... you see it was a short cut to his work... mind you the ticks on that path... remind me to ask you for the recipe... you use butter, don't you? But butter... 'but butter'... I like that... it's so expensive...when you can get it... anyway, those kids of mine... thank you, Nobby, please fuga lapa lo ma pot... basop... haikona enza lo ma spilling... I can just picture them... but fancy fighting over Blossom's leftovers... half a cup of tepid tea... alliteration... still in his thermos flask, and maybe a stale egg sandwich... I mean... you could have knocked me down with a feather."

Nobuhle returned to the kitchen and hovered. That bell always put her into a nervous state. She had never got used to it. It reminded her of the bell in the Shu-Shine bus that took her to Kezi, the one the passengers rang when they needed to relieve themselves, or be dropped off. And that reminded her of the day she was brutally raped and left for dead, dangling from that marula tree. The smell of the fruit still made her nauseous, and the madam insisted on making her collect it by the basketful, in order to make her prize-winning jelly.

185

Maye, but that was a terrible time, right from the first road block just outside Bulawayo. Every few kilometres they had been stopped and searched, not by police but by soldiers. Anyone carrying food was accused of supporting dissidents. Their food was confiscated and they were clapped – even elderly women – by the soldiers. Luckily for Nobuhle and one or two others, their bags of mealie meal had been stashed on the roof of the bus underneath some corrugated iron sheets, and they went unnoticed. By the time they got to Kezi there was not a single young man left on the bus.

At her family home in Donkwe Donkwe village there was mayhem. All the men including her father and her fifteen year old son had been shot dead, accused of concealing firearms. The remaining women and children were on the point of starvation, so Nobuhle's bag of mealie meal was most welcome. But it did not do Nobuhle any good.

On her second day home, while she was cooking a communal meal in a large, battered enamel pot, some drunken soldiers wearing red berets arrived and accused her of feeding dissidents. They ordered her to strip naked, tied her wrists with electric cable, and hoisted her so that she dangled from a tree branch, her big toes just touching the rotting fruit on the ground below. The soldiers had great fun spinning her like a top and then raping her – sometimes from the front, sometimes from the back – over and over again. There must have been about ten or twelve of them. The other women and children had fled into the bush, and this angered the soldiers so much that they set fire to all the huts. They lost interest in Nobuhle when she lost consciousness, and left her hanging there.

When the villagers returned, they brought her down from the tree, washed her and helped her get dressed. When the life returned to her fingers and she was strong enough to walk, she made her way to St

Joseph's Mission in Matobo South, and there she was cared for, and there she remained until she felt strong enough to return, on foot, through the bush, to Bulawayo. The madam took her back without much complaining.

The bell rang. "Nobby, buya tata lo ma things but yega lo ma shortbread ka lo Missis Mabel, iswili?"

"Yes, Madam." Nobuhle came in with a tray and cleared the table of everything but the plate of shortbread. She was dressed in a floral patterned maid's uniform with matching apron and doek. She returned to the kitchen and hovered.

"I simply don't know where I... where Blossom and I went wrong with those children – one's an alcoholic, the other's a lesbian. I mean, can you credit it... 'credit it'... I like that." The others had heard it all before. They were patient with Mimi. Fortunately she started a choking fit, from a crumb of shortbread, which had gone down the wrong way, and this gave them the opportunity to get down to the real business of the gathering, which was to read Ethel's play – a doggerel adaptation of one of Kipling's "Just So Stories".

"Kipling's out of favour, you know," remarked Olga.

Mimi had recovered from her fit: "Which white male writer isn't? Ask my daughter, if she'll bother to talk to you. Even Shakespeare... bardicide... well I'm a bardolater and proud of it... I don't know... I really have no idea where we went wrong. We were always there for our children... the cakes I made for their birthdays! One year it was a steam engine for Cornwallis and a sunflower for Ladybird; another year it was a motor car for Cornwallis and a Heidi doll for Ladybird...." Mimi lowered her head and examined the bunion on her left thumb. Her friends gave sympathetic murmurs – they all had stories to tell. "You could have knocked me down with a feather when she told me she never wanted to speak to me again. Once a year she comes home and stays with the girl in the servant's quarters... brings her all sorts of gifts from Sweden... she still doesn't realise how much Nobby hates those sweets that taste like Scrubbs Ammonia... and those pickled herrings, which I would give my back teeth... well, dentures.... As for that no-good son of mine... how old is he? – 48 and still living at home. All those wasted years at university. He does nothing... sits in his room all day and smokes and drinks and listens to opera..."

"But Mimi, he got badly damaged in the war."

"It was his decision to join the R.L.I."

"He would have been called up, anyway."

"What about his garden? Doesn't he love gardening?"

"Yes... there is that... but-"

Listen, let's change the subject, shall we? Ethel, let's read."

"Yes, no... I was thinking of Cornwallis's little garden. He does make an effort in that regard... he has these beautiful little plants... such a fresh shade of green... that remind me of miniature cabbage trees... did you know that dassies browse on their leaves... you should see the jars upon jars of rolled mops, which she forces down that poor girl's throat... did you ever try Sapphics, Olga? Maybe we should-"

"Mimi! Please!"

"Oh, I'm sorry, so sorry...."

3

Dr L.T. "Bug" Swinburne, was lying on her Gogo's creaky iron bed, its four legs propped on concrete breeze bricks (a tried and tested defence against tokoloshes), its uneven mattress prickly with coir. She was reading through her paper, due be published in the journal of African

Cultural Studies, and entitled "Troping the Trope: Vaginis-music in Yvonne Vera's *The Stone Virgins*". She was still simmering with anger at her brother's cynical dismissal of her analysis of the beautifully horrific scene where Sibaso, the Ndebele dissident, after beheading Tenjiwe and then dancing with her body, turns to her sister, Nonceba, and spends an entire chapter raping and mutilating her in a choreography that would have made Nijinski's knees buckle.

"You know what Primo Levi would have called that," he had said.

"What?"

"'Aesthetic affectation'."

"He would. He is a man."

"Was. He committed suicide."

"Why don't you take his cue, Cornwallis?"

"I'm already dead."

"You reek of self-pity."

"And you reek of sanctimony."

"Fuck you!"

"Jesus, why vaginas? Why not something less in-your-face like cracks or slits or seams…"

"They've all been taken."

"By your fellow academics?"

"Look, it's not just vaginas; it's a combination of 'vaginismus', which is a painful spasmodic contraction, and 'music', which is one of Vera's privileged tropes."

"Oh gawd!"

This recall of the altercation kept imposing itself between her cutting-edge persona and the 3 000 word paper.

Once a year she returned to the country of her birth, Zimbabwe, to visit the woman who had reared her and her pathetic older brother.

189

Gogo's real name was Nobuhle Xaba and she had worked for the Swinburne family since 1960, the year Cornwallis was born. She came from the Donkwe Donkwe area near Kezi. She used to go home fairly regularly, until the troubles began in the 80s. In April, 1984, she responded to a distress call from a family member (Miss Ladybird had just returned to her university in South Africa) and quickly boarded a bus for Kezi. A month later she had not returned, and the Swinburnes thought she had abandoned them. Another month passed, and another; then, one day, she turned up at their gate looking ill and miserable enough for Mimi not to berate her. Gogo wouldn't go into details but, clearly, she'd been seriously traumatized. She was put on light chores and fed huge helpings of Mimi's famous puddings, until she became strong enough to resume her normal duties. She never went back to Donkwe Donkwe.

It was at the University of Natal, studying for a BA in English and History, that Bug (she hated her given names, Ladybird Titania) became politicised. The shock of realising that she had grown up in a sub-culture that regarded black people as inferior to white people, and treated them as such, turned her overnight against her own people, her family in particular. She began a series of love affairs designed to cut her parents to the quick – with black men, with known communists, with what her father called dykes; and she became promiscuous. She cut off all her hair and she pierced her nostrils with a sliver of bone. She ceased to keep herself clean and began to stink, according to her brother, like rotting butternut. She read Doris Lessing, Simone de Beauvoir, Germaine Greer, Marylin French... and it dawned on her that women were probably just as oppressed as black men, though not in the same league as black women, who suffered the double bind of racial as well as gender oppression – hence her obsessive interest, two decades later, in writers like Yvonne Vera. Her sick-in-the-head brother insisted on calling the great novelist a Canadian.

"She wasn't a Canadian, you fuckwit, she was Zimbabwean."

"She had Canadian citizenship."

"So?"

"So, Zimbabweans aren't allowed dual citizenship. It's a jailable offence."

They saw each other only for a few days a year; and they spent it quarrelling. But at least Bug talked to her brother. She completely ignored poor Mimi, and spent most of her time with Gogo in the servant's quarters. Friends of the family were convinced that it was Bug's behaviour which sent her father, Blossom, to an early grave.

Bug was simultaneously re-reading her analysis of the rape scene and smarting at her brother's comments. While she saw it as balletic, Terpsichorean, he called it hokey-cokey: "You put your left knee in, you take your left knee out, you put your left knee in and you wiggle it about..."

"The trouble with you bigoted white men is that you can conceive of history only in linear time. From head to toe you are hierarchical, and you place yourselves firmly on the top. Well, my friend, your days are numbered.... Can't you see that Yvonne Vera subverts those notions?"

Can't *you* see that Yvonne Vera's so-called novels are typological? She herself was an academic steeped in the same theories as the incestuous band of PhDs she wrote for. She knew exactly what postmodernist feminists thrive on: aporias, tropes, subalternity, liminality...fucksake!"

191

Nobuhle arrived, tired out after a day's housekeeping, and Bug slid off her bed. "Gogo, come and lie down for a while. I'll make you a nice cup of tea."

Nobuhle knew not to argue with the Picanin Missis. She gave her a smile, climbed onto the bed – she knew what was coming next – and made her tackies available for Bug to untie and gently remove. "Shall I give your feet a rub?"

"Thank you, Bugi. The Madam is cross today."

"What now?"

"She says the other Madams tease her. She..." Nobuhle broke off to stifle a giggle... "she says they say her face is like other madams' bums."

"What?" Bug beamed as she pressed her thumbs into the soles of her Gogo's worn out feet. "Because she talks shit."

Nobuhle winced as Bug's thumbs suddenly behaved as if they were at her mother's throat. "Sorry, Gogo. Let me put some camphor cream on your heels."

"I only have Vaseline. There, by the window ledge."

"That should work." She fetched the jar of Vaseline, opened it, scooped some grease with her left index finger, closed the jar, returned it to the window ledge, and returned to her Gogo's feet. "My people," she sighed; "and the governing episteme is almost as bad. Why? Because African nationalism is patriarchal."

"I do not understand."

"Men, Gogo, amadoda!"

"Oh! By the way!" She laughed.

"It's not funny, you know." Then she thought, I must work on this Manichaean tendency of mine, learn like Yvonne Vera to insinuate the alterity of the voiceless into hegemonic space. Gogo's pads were as hard and as rough as Brazil nut shells. "Men, obsessed with virginity and rape. Contradictory bastards. Now, let's have some tea and some of that nice pickled herring I brought you from-"

"Tsss, Bugi, it is hurting!"

"Oh, I'm sorry, Gogo, so sorry…."

Printed in the United States
By Bookmasters